THE FINAL CUT

ALSO BY DENIS MARKELL

Click Here to Start

The Game Masters of Garden Place

The Ghost in Apartment 2R

THE FINAL CUT

DENIS MARKELL

DELACORTE PRESS

Text copyright © 2022 by Denis Markell
Jacket art copyright © 2022 by Louie Chin

Visit us on the Web! rhcbooks.com

Educators and librarians, for a variety of teaching tools, visit us at RHTeachersLibrarians.com

Library of Congress Cataloging-in-Publication Data
Names: Markell, Denis, author.
Title: The final cut / Denis Markell.
Description: First edition. | New York: Delacorte Press, [2022] |
Audience: Ages 10 and up. | Summary: When seventh-grader Alex is stuck taking Film, he has to learn to work with two very different students to make the movie they want to make, even as someone tries to stop them.
Identifiers: LCCN 2020056122 (print) | LCCN 2020056123 (ebook) |
ISBN 978-0-593-18066-2 (hardcover) | ISBN 978-0-593-18067-9 (library binding) | ISBN 978-0-593-18068-6 (ebook)
Subjects: CYAC: Motion pictures—Production and direction—Fiction. | Middle schools—Fiction. | Schools—Fiction. | Best friends—Fiction. | Friendship—Fiction. | Mystery and detective stories.
Classification: LCC PZ7.M339453 Fin 2022 (print) | LCC PZ7.M339453 (ebook) | DDC [Fic]—dc23

The text of this book is set in 11-point Amasis MT Pro.
Interior design by Andrea Lau

Printed in the United States of America
10 9 8 7 6 5 4 3 2 1
First Edition

THE FINAL CUT

CHAPTER 1

The Hero's Journey Begins with a Thud

"Call me Xan."

I smile my coolest smile at the mirror.

Okay, if my voice hadn't cracked, it probably would have sounded cooler.

And the expression on my face looked less like "I'm the most chill kid in seventh grade" and more "I have digestive issues that need to be taken care of immediately."

But other than that, I'm pretty satisfied.

Let's face it, seventh grade is a big deal.

The truth is, I had hoped that sixth grade would be a big deal.

A few years ago, my older cousin Leo, who goes to public school on Long Island, told me about how they had a whole graduation after fifth grade, and sixth grade meant moving to a whole different school, like it was the start of something new and fresh.

But I go to this weird private school where there's no fuss made about changing grades. There's no new start, just the same kids who've known you since the first grade when someone caught you eating your booger or something.

(For the record, that totally did *not* happen to me. It was another kid. I was just using it as an example.)

But this *is* the beginning of the school year. A fresh start, right?

No more boring Alex Davis.

Time to introduce my friends and fellow students to Xan Davis, the awesome kid who went to skate camp, becoming a legend in the process.

So they don't need to know that I became a legend by spraining my ankle the first day of camp and spending the rest of the time there taking videos of the other skaters.

I might not have learned how to do a kickflip or a grind or an ollie (I did master the Biebelheimer, which is just a sweet-looking way to put down your board), but I ended up getting really good at editing videos of the other kids.

Ranger, who was *definitely* the coolest kid there, decided that "Alex" was nerdy, so he dubbed me "Xan" and it stuck.

And now here I am, back home in Brooklyn Heights, embarking on the adventure of seventh grade.

I inspect my outfit. On the one hand, you want to look good on your first day, but on the other, you don't want to look like you tried too hard. I have on my SK8 KAMP T-shirt and cargo shorts.

Alex Davis wouldn't have the nerve to wear this to school. But Xan definitely does. I pull on my Vans (the same style that Ranger wore) and look in the mirror next to the front door one last time.

I muss my hair. For that casual, "I don't care" look.

My mom comes up and hugs me.

"You look so grown up!" she exclaims, and promptly licks her palm and applies said wet disgusting hand to my hair, dorkifying it with one stroke.

"Mom! Stop!"

Mom sighs. "Alex, you—"

"Xan!"

"Sorry, *Xan*," my mom says, reaching for my hair, "but you don't want to start seventh grade with bedhead, do you?"

I grab my backpack and push open the front door. "I don't want to start seventh grade by being late either. Bye."

From the kitchen a yell. "Mooooom!"

My little sister, Violet, who is also starting school today.

But it's only third grade, so really, who cares?

Mom grabs me and kisses me. "Have a great day! I hope you get all your electives!"

I head out onto the street and give her a quick wave goodbye.

Truthfully, I am a little anxious about the electives. At my school, you don't get your schedule until the first day.

From what I understand, this is supposed to stop what my

mom and dad call "a certain type of parent" from phoning the head of school and screaming because their precious little gift to the world didn't get their preferred teacher or elective.

Which might have been true in theory, but seriously, do you think this actually stops any of them? All it means is that we don't find out which classes we have until the very last minute.

I should explain that this is one of the big deals about seventh grade at Saint Anselm's. It's the first year you can pick certain classes for yourself—electives.

There's all sorts of cool stuff being offered, from studying mushrooms in nearby Prospect Park to fashion design to folk dancing (okay, not my thing, but there are kids in my class who live for that kind of stuff).

What is stressing me out is that the *one* elective I really, really want—Game Theory: Video Game History and Design—is also the most popular (I know, go figure, right?). There are always more kids who sign up for it than there are spots in the class, so it's kind of a lottery. I won't know until I see my schedule if I'm one of the lucky ones who got it.

I'm thinking about how awesome it would be to actually design and make my own video game (and during school too!) when I hear a familiar voice.

"Alex! Hello? I've been waiting like five minutes here."

Lexie Mizell has lived across the street from me ever since we were in kindergarten. We used to walk to school with our moms, but since last year, we've been walking together.

"Call me Xan," I say.

Lexie takes a moment to let that sink in. Then she bursts out laughing. "Call you *what*?"

"Ummm . . . Xan . . ." I can feel the coolness leaking out of me like air escaping a balloon.

Minus the farting noise.

At least for now.

"Wait," Lexie says, trying to catch her breath. "Is it spelled with an *X* or a *Z*?"

I start down the street, not answering.

"That is the *stupidest* thing I've ever heard," Lexie calls after me. "Hey! Wait up!"

I'm pretty sure my face is redder than Mario's hat (yes, I have video games on the brain right now). "Look, I thought you wanted to get to school."

Lexie catches up with me at the light. "Alex, hold up. You *cannot* be serious about having everybody call you Xan all of a sudden. It's just so . . . *not you*."

"You don't know me," I say. "A lot has changed over the summer. And of course it's spelled with an *X* since my name is Ale*Xan*der. Duh."

Lexie shrugs. Then she looks at my outfit. "Oh jeez, Alex—I mean *Xan*. What are you dressed up as?"

"I'm just wearing my skate clothes," I explain patiently.

"So . . . if you're such a cool skater dude now, where is your board?" Lexie asks.

"Well . . . it's at home. It needs to be repaired. I messed it up doing ollies."

"Oh brother," Lexie says, shaking her head.

I try a different approach. "At least I made an effort to wear something nice for the first day of school."

Lexie, unlike me, hasn't changed a bit over the summer. She's wearing the same ratty *Powerpuff Girls* T-shirt and pink jeans that she rotates with a series of other anime and vintage cartoon clothing throughout the year. She's been wearing the same stuff for so long, I know them by heart. And she's wearing her hair the same way, pulled back from her face and held in a ponytail with an old plastic Pokémon barrette.

Lexie snorts. "Like I'm going to take fashion advice from a poser like you."

But I can see that her face has gotten red too.

We arrive at the front door of our school, where kids from the various classes are all bunched up together.

There's an explosion of high-pitched screams and giggles as a group of girls hug and jump up and down as if they've just found a long-lost relative instead of having spent all last month in their summer homes together out on Long Island.

Guys, of course, are cooler.

Brandon, one of my buddies, sidles up. "'Sup, Alex?"

"Hey, Brandon."

"He's not Alex anymore," Lexie feels the need to say. "He's Xan now. The cool skater kid."

Brandon shakes his head. "Dude, no way. Xan? That is so wrong."

I am about to explain why Xan is actually a very cool name when Brandon calls out to two boys passing by, holding skateboards.

"Yo, Dylan! Lucas! Alex wants to be called Xan now!"

Lucas nods. "Wow. That is some name. Very cool."

He then pokes Dylan in the ribs. "We should all change our names! You can be Dill! Like the pickle!"

Dylan smacks Lucas in the rib cage. "Yeah, and you can be Puke. Pukus."

I decide to get in on the fun. "And Brandon could be Bran Muffin!"

They all stare at me.

"That's a stupid name," Lucas declares.

"Almost as stupid as Xan!" Brandon says, and they all laugh.

Lexie lets me off the hook. "You guys get your schedules already?"

"They haven't opened the doors yet," Dylan says, twirling on his board in ways I can only dream of.

Just then, there's a commotion and kids of all ages start crowding around the entrance.

"Guess they just did," Lexie says.

I go for the kill. "Good one, Einstein."

Lexie rolls her eyes. "Ooh, what a burn. That's like from fourth grade."

Cedric, the security guard who is like six feet infinity, stands blocking the doorway.

"Welcome back!" he booms in his deep, melodic voice. "Now line up nice before I start hurting people!"

We all know that Cedric would never hurt a kid (he might yell if you run across the street without looking), but we all quiet down and get ourselves into something kind of resembling a line.

As we watch the younger kids file in, I think, *This is it. The moment of truth. Where I'll see if this will be a year filled with promise, filled with video games and adventure, or a waking nightmare where I'll long for the sweet release of death.*

That last part is actually from a story I wrote for sixth-grade English.

My teacher Mr. Halverson wrote three exclamation points next to it and said it was "hilarious!" So I thought I'd use it here.

We enter the lobby of the school and see the familiar long tables set up, one per grade. There are three teachers at each table, with the letters of the alphabet split among them. I run to A–F and find my favorite history teacher, Mrs. Kantor, waiting with a big smile.

Mrs. Kantor shuffles through the papers in front of her and pulls out my schedule. "Hey, Alex! Welcome back! Looks like you're stuck with me again this year."

"Wow! I'm so stoked!" I say, meaning it. She made fifth-grade history interesting, doing stuff like dressing up as Abraham Lincoln and letting us reenact famous battles with Lego Minifigs.

I hold my breath as my eyes race down the page.

History with Kantor.

English with Mr. Sackler, who is supposed to be good.

Intro to Algebra, science, Biology 1 . . .

Yeah, yeah, yeah.

Then I see it.

My elective.

Pottery with Graciela Livonia.

Pottery?

As the room begins to swim around me, I hear Lexie's triumphant voice from down the table:

"Game Theory! *Yes!*"

CHAPTER 2

Alex (the) Potter and the Half-Baked Elective

I am still trying to process all this when I dimly hear Mrs. Kantor's voice.

"Alex? If there's a problem, you need to see Mrs. Hannigan."

I look up to see her kind eyes and sympathetic smile.

"But . . . but . . . ," I stammer.

"Alex, please." Mrs. Kantor gestures, and I realize there are a lot of ticked off students lined up behind me. I wander out of line in a daze.

Pottery?

We were asked to pick three electives, and we would definitely be given one of our three. I never signed up for pottery.

I push through a crowd of high-fiving kids who have clearly gotten their first choices.

I hate them with the cold, hard fury of a thousand dead stars.

(Yes, that's also from my paper for Mr. Halverson. He wrote *A little too over the top?* next to that line, but I like it.)

In the corner, with a dozen or so kids crowded around her, is Mrs. Hannigan, who is in charge of the sixth and seventh grades. I know her already, since she taught my math class last year, so I feel I have a good chance of getting what I want.

"But you *have* to!" Persephone Chang is wailing. Tears are pouring out of her eyes.

Mrs. Hannigan looks unmoved. "Just give it a chance. I would change it if I could—"

"But Mr. Melrose *hates* me!" Persephone sobs.

I should mention that Persephone is by far the best actress in our class. She doesn't always know when to stop performing, but I have to admit this is an amazing display.

"He doesn't hate you," Mrs. Hannigan says evenly, handing Persephone what looks like her fifth tissue. "He's actually quite a fan of your work."

Persephone brightens. "Really?"

"He just wishes you'd bring the same . . . passion . . . to science that you do to theater."

"That's not possible," Persephone says. "I mean, theater is my life."

Mrs. Hannigan scratches her head. "How about this. I bet you could *act* like you're interested."

Persephone thinks for a minute. "It's a challenge. But I accept."

With a flourish, Persephone grabs her schedule from Mrs. Hannigan and flounces off.

Having vanquished Persephone, Mrs. Hannigan takes a deep breath. She then turns to me and brightens. "Alex! Welcome back!"

There is a "Finally! Someone sane!" tone to her voice, which I take as a good sign.

Before I can answer her, there is shouting from behind me.

"Hey, *Xan*! *Xan the man!*"

It's Mateo and Nathan, two of the bigger jerks in our class. Not really mean, but the kind of kids who think they are funnier than everyone else.

Obviously word of my new name has gotten around.

Mateo pushes me out of the way and leans on the table. "Hey, Mrs. Hannigan! Haven't you heard? His name isn't Alex anymore! It's Xan!"

"Xan the man!" Nathan crows. As if it's twice as funny if he says it twice.

Mrs. Hannigan has probably heard everything in her years at Saint Anselm's. I know there's an eighth grader who decided to change his name from Eric to StormRider (I am totally not kidding), and in our class a kid named Ralph is just known by his initials, RPG.

"Is that why you wanted to see me?" Mrs. Hannigan asks. "To change your name?"

"Um, no, Alex is fine," I say. "It's more . . . this . . ."

I point to the elective box on my schedule.

"Yes . . . pottery. I know that wasn't your first choice."

"It wasn't like my *fifteenth* choice," I say. "I can't understand why I was put in it."

Mrs. Hannigan scrunches up her face. "That doesn't make sense. Let's look at your list."

She turns to a box of index cards, the ones we filled out last spring.

"We'll get this sorted out," she says.

Mrs. Hannigan is a good person. I know as soon as she sees that I didn't put down pottery, she'll make this right.

Her eyes brighten. "Ah! Here it is!" She pulls out my card and peers at it.

"Hmm. Yep. You wrote pottery as your second choice, Alex."

She hands me the card.

Okay, I kind of rushed to finish it so I could hand it in early, and my handwriting isn't great under the best of circumstances, but still.

I show her. "It says *poetry*." One of the electives was Poetry and Images in Rap Music from the Seventies Until Today.

I guess I should have written out the full name.

Mrs. Hannigan peers at the word. "*Poetry?* You have to

admit it looks like *pottery*. You really need to work on your handwriting."

"Agreed. But I don't want to take pottery," I say as calmly as I can. "I wanted to take Game Theory."

"Everybody wanted to take Game Theory," Mrs. Hannigan sighs. "There's no way I can get you into that. And the second most popular elective is the rap music one."

"How about my third choice?" I ask as visions of wet, gloppy clay dance before my eyes.

Mrs. Hannigan consults my card. "I'm sorry, Alex, Graphic Novels is also completely filled."

"But I don't want to take pottery!" I say, my lower lip trembling. I'm no Persephone, but I can let my emotions get the best of me if it means guilting Mrs. Hannigan into bending the rules.

"Alex, I wish I could give every student their first choice, but that's just not possible."

I wipe my eyes. "It's not my fault! I wrote *poetry*!"

Mrs. Hannigan pleads with me. "Why don't you *try* pottery? You might find you love it. It happens all the time."

"I'm not going to love pottery," I say, "and I think it stinks that I didn't get into any of my choices because someone else made a mistake."

The bell rings for first period. Mrs. Hannigan looks relieved. "Alex, I promise I'll do everything I can to get you into an elective you'll like. Let me ask around and I'll talk to you after assembly."

Assembly is two periods away. That's where the whole middle school meets and announcements are made.

English is first period, and then history.

And assuming I can trust Mrs. Hannigan, my being forced to take pottery will be *history* too.

CHAPTER 3

Mrs. Hannigan to the Rescue, I Guess?

First and second periods are the usual first-day-of-school "Here's what we're going to study this year, and here's a handout, and I am going to go on and on about the challenges of seventh grade and why it's important to turn in your homework on time blah blah blah . . ." speech, which they seem to give word for word every year, except for changing the grade.

Mrs. Kantor's is funnier, because she puts in jokes, like "If you see a comment on your paper that says 'How many energy drinks did you consume before writing this?' I am not actually asking that question but rather suggesting that your writing needs clarification." Mr. Sackler is a little drier, and it seems he's as bored giving the speech as we are hearing it.

To be honest, I kind of zone out during both periods, since I'm really anxious to hear what Mrs. Hannigan is going to say after assembly.

Just as Mrs. Kantor is giving us our very first history assignment of seventh grade, the bell rings and we head downstairs for assembly, which is held in the big open lobby area where everyone can basically squeeze in to hear the announcements. There is a big staircase covered with red carpet leading from the lobby to the floor where all the administrators are. Kids are sprawled all over it, chattering and catching up from the summer.

I find Lexie and Brandon hanging out at the bottom with several other kids in our grade. I kind of wish one of them was in my humanities classes (that's what we call English and history) so I'd have someone whose notes I could borrow, but the upside is that I don't need to have competitive Lexie answering every question before I can even raise my hand.

It turns out Brandon got into Game Theory as well.

"Game Theory is going to rock so hard!" Brandon says loudly. "Oh, *sorry, Xan,* didn't see you there."

"I don't know why everybody is giving me such grief about wanting a cooler name," I grumble.

Lexie side-eyes me. "There are plenty of cool people named Alex, Alex."

"Name one."

I should know better.

"Let's see," Lexie begins. "There's Alex Rider—kid secret

agent in those books. He's pretty cool. Alex Rodriguez, legendary Yankee—"

"With the nickname A-Rod," I remind her.

"Alex Trebek," Brandon adds. "Now, *he* was a legend."

"Anyway, *your* name is Alexandra," I say to Lexie. "How come you get to have a nickname and I don't?"

Lexie shakes her head. "Alex, I have been Lexie since I was a baby. I didn't just randomly decide one day to change what people call me."

"It wasn't random," I say. "I was *given* the name at skate camp."

Lexie bites her lip. I can tell she wants to laugh *so bad.* "Ohhh right. *Skate camp.* So who gave you this name? Like the counselors or something?"

"Actually, it was like the best skater in the whole camp."

"And what was his name?" Brandon snorts. "Scooter?"

Now I'm getting mad. "Actually, it was Ranger. And that's his real name, Ranger Basinger."

Lexie nods. "Uh-huh. Wow. With a name like that, how did he not end up at Saint Anselm's?"

It's true. We have a lot of creative parents here, so we get used to having kids named Loki and ClearWater and everything in between.

"You just proved my point!" I say triumphantly. "Xan is a perfect Saint Anselm's name! Why is it so funny to you?"

"Because you. Are. So. *Not.* A. Xan, Alex. You are an Alex, Alex." Lexie answers with so much pity in her voice that I want to hit her.

Except then she would hit me back, and she is definitely stronger than I am.

"Okay. I get it. I'm an Alex."

"Thank you," Lexie says, giving me a genuine smile. "I'm just trying to save you from total humiliation on your first day of seventh grade."

Brandon is ready to move on. "Speaking of total humiliation, just wait until I design my video game in Game Theory. It's going to destroy you."

For some reason, I say something I know is total BS.

"That's another thing, Lexie," I grouse. "Why are *you* taking Game Theory? You don't even like video games."

Lexie gives me her patented "Are you out of your mind?" look. "Are you out of your mind?" (Told you.) "I am totally into video games. As you well know, considering I beat you at *Super Smash Bros.* eight out of ten games whenever we play, although we haven't played since that time you threw your controller at me and I don't like sore losers."

"You are such a drama queen," I say. "I didn't throw it. It slipped."

"Dude, you totally threw it. I was there," Brandon reminds me.

"Shh. Assembly's starting," I say, glad to end the conversation.

Mrs. Hannigan has made her way to the top of the stairs where everyone can see her and is clapping her hands.

"Welcome! Welcome back!" she says, and everyone quiets

down. Having a loud voice is definitely a must if you're going to be the head of a middle school.

"Hello to all you brand-new sixth graders!" Mrs. Hannigan begins.

There is an obnoxious level of whooping and screaming.

"Sixth graders are *the worst*," Lexie says.

"You said it," I agree.

The fact that just three months ago we were in the sixth grade is not important. We were different. Nothing like this group of losers. (Yeah, I know the eighth graders say the same thing about us.)

"And of course, I can't forget my seventh-grade posse!" Mrs. Hannigan adds.

Obviously we have to make more noise than the sixth graders, just to let them know who is in charge here. So we all yell and cheer, even though it was super cringey for Mrs. Hannigan to call us her "posse."

Why do grown-ups do that?

I mean, not just the corny ones like Mr. Jackson, who teaches rec arts (that's what Saint Anselm's actually calls gym; I am completely serious), who says "'Sup, dude!" totally unironically.

But Mrs. Hannigan is cool. Especially since she is going to get me into an elective I want. Maybe she'll kick Lexie out of Game Theory!

That isn't going to happen. But it gives me an idea.

"Hey, Lexie, you like making pottery, right?"

"That's kind of random, isn't it?" Lexie asks. "Like, hey, speaking of naked mole rats . . ."

"Seriously. I hear the pottery elective is amazing."

Lexie's eyes widen. "Really? You think I should take it instead of Game Theory?"

"I dunno," I say. "You might not be able to get in. It's like the most popular elective this year."

"Wow. You know . . . maybe I can talk to Mrs. Hannigan about it," Lexie says.

Brandon turns around. "Ask her about what?"

"About who the most pathetic seventh grader is, because I nominate Alex Davis. Did you actually think you could get me to transfer out of Game Theory and into pottery?" Lexie asks, laughing so loudly that Mrs. Hannigan stops the whole assembly and asks her what is so funny.

"Nothing, Mrs. Hannigan. Alex was just telling me a joke."

Mrs. Hannigan glares at me. "I'd appreciate it if you'd listen to what I'm saying up here, Alex, unless you think jokes are more important."

"I'm sorry, Mrs. Hannigan," I say, apologizing for something I didn't even do.

Now you know why I don't want Lexie in my English and history classes.

So I listen as Mrs. Hannigan makes announcements about stuff I already know, like how seventh graders are allowed to go outside for lunch, instead of having to eat in the lunchroom, and how we're to understand that when we *are* outside, we're representing the school, and none of us want to have people saying "There go those obnoxious Saint Anselm's kids" when they see us, do we?

Nathan lets out a whoop, and Mrs. Hannigan gives him a look so hard it sticks in his throat.

"Do you have something to say, Nathan?" she asks.

"Nope. Just coughing," Nathan says, snickering.

After what seems like an hour of similar dumb things (did the sixth graders *really* not know that all homework had to be handed in on time? They look pretty dense, but I assume even they have some idea of how this "going to school" thing works), the bell rings and Mrs. Hannigan sends everyone on to third period.

Everyone but me and two other kids.

Bethany Silverman is hopping from foot to foot as Mrs. Hannigan tells her, "Good news, Bethany! Someone has dropped out of pottery! You're all set!"

Bethany breaks into an enormous grin and she shouts "*Yes!* Thank you, Mrs. Hannigan! You are the *best*!"

Who knew that dropping out of pottery would make someone so happy?

Bethany skips off, and Stuart Dyckman is informed that sadly, the percussion class is totally filled. But Mrs. Hannigan can squeeze him into the jazz ensemble, where he can play drums.

Stuart nods. "That works for me. Good deal."

Now it's my turn. Mrs. Hannigan glances down at her pad. I feel like the Scarecrow in *The Wizard of Oz*, about to get his brain from the Wizard.

Yeah, I know he didn't actually get a brain—he was just made to understand that he was smarter than he thought. We talked about that scene in writing class last year.

"Okay, here's what I was able to do. Game Theory is oversized as it is, but I was able to get you into an elective I think you'll like. And no arguing. You're going to accept this, right?"

"Does it involve dancing?" I ask. "I'm not dancing."

"No dancing," Mrs. Hannigan promises. She hands me a card.

I turn it over.

The Moving Image: Film Studies 1. Pablo Rosenstein, room 5-2.

I open my mouth to say something, but Mrs. Hannigan holds up her hand.

"The next words out of your mouth better be 'thank you,' Alex Davis."

I am about to say "Thank you, Alex Davis," but I know now is not the time for that sort of thing.

"Thanks, Mrs. Hannigan. This is much better."

"Now get up there. I have a feeling you're going to love this class," Mrs. Hannigan says.

I sprint up the stairs to the fifth floor and find myself outside room 5-2.

Who knows? Maybe this will be better than Game Theory. At least Lexie won't be here.

I turn the doorknob and, filled with happy anticipation, open the door.

Then I walk in and my heart sinks to the floor.

CHAPTER 4

Lights, Camera, Action . . . Pablo Rosenstein!

Maybe my heart doesn't *literally* sink to the floor (kind of a gross image, when you think about it), but I wince when the first thing I hear is "Pew! Pew! Pew!" and see obnoxious Nathan and Mateo running around the room reenacting their favorite scene from *Star Wars*.

An entire year with these two. Great. Just great. Thankfully, they seem to have forgotten about the whole "Xan" thing since I saw them this morning. That's all I need right now.

Nathan bumps into three girls who are like triplets: Jojo, Oona, and Joie. They are on the gymnastics team and dress totally alike and wear their hair the same, finish each other's sentences, and are so scary (they could totally beat up any boy in the class) that even Nathan mumbles "Sorry" and slinks off before diving below a desk and resuming his obnoxious "Pew! Pew!" thing.

I try to see if anyone in the class is worth sitting next to. There is the nerd camp—I'm sorry, but these guys get together on weekends and play some game where you make up stories about dragons and wizards and cast spells and the more I'm talking about it the cooler it sounds so I think I'll stop.

That kid nicknamed RPG is here with his pal Noel, who was in my history class last year and would *not* shut up, so this is going to be fun. At least their other friend Cammi is really quiet. That's a plus.

Then in the front row, I see her.

Sitting by herself, making the whole class suddenly seem 100% cooler, is Priti Sharma.

If you're from India, or if you have any friends who are, you know already that Priti is actually a common name. But most people don't know that, so when they hear her name, they think it's a nickname or something. We've been in school together since fourth grade, so I'm used to her name, but it must be hard for her to deal with idiots who make comments about it.

I don't think it helps (maybe it does?) that Priti is really *pretty.* At least most of the girls in the class seem to think so. Don't go by me. I hear it all the time in the hall with them all oohing and aahing over pictures from her Instagram. She's also from a really rich family and is always going on exotic trips and posing in front of famous landmarks holding some expensive purse or something.

I only know about the Instagram stuff because I overheard my mom and Lexie's mom talking about it last summer. They were going on about how kids grow up too fast these days and Lexie's mom showed my mom Priti's Instagram and my mom shook her head and said, "Wow. She looks like she's sixteen." Which I would have thought was a compliment, but the way she said it I know it wasn't.

Priti is literally the coolest person in middle school, and not only is she cool, but she's smart too. There used to be two of them—this girl Isabel Archer was her best friend, and they were kind of the brains of the school (and we're supposedly a school for gifted children, although looking at Nathan and Mateo, I have serious questions about that) but then Isabel moved away over the summer and now Priti is kind of by herself as the Smartest Kid in the Seventh Grade.

I don't dare sit next to her, because . . . I can't quite explain it. I think I'm afraid she'll act all nice to me and ask my name and I'll have to remind her we were in English and math together for three years but she just didn't notice.

Or worse, Nathan or Mateo will start in with the "Xan" stuff and she'll say "I thought your name was Alex" and I'd have to tell her everything, which, I mean, I would rather cut off my arm and eat it.

So I sit a few seats away. She's busy scrolling through her phone anyway, so it's not like she notices.

So maybe this *is* a cooler class than I thought. Unless she also wrote *pottery* by mistake. That's impossible, since I don't think Priti Sharma has made a single mistake in her entire life.

Things have moved on in *Star Wars,* and Mateo has become Darth Vader swinging his lightsaber and is making a kind of *WOOOW* sound (I have to admit he's pretty good at *Star Wars* sound effects) when he backs right into this person entering the room.

At first I think it's another student because of how he's dressed—in jeans and a T-shirt. Then I see the scruffy beard and books under his arm (actually, now they're on the floor since Mateo knocked into him) and realize that this has to be our *teacher.*

Pablo Rosenstein definitely has that "cool teacher" vibe. I just hope he won't say something like "Mr. Rosenstein is my father. Call me Pablo!" or call us "dudes."

Those guys are always trying so hard it's kind of sad. Pablo just looks like a teacher who assumes that we'll call him by his first name.

Pablo has long wavy hair that kind of sticks up in the air and then falls back. He has wire-rimmed glasses and a vintage watch of some kind.

I would bet money he writes with a fountain pen.

Mateo mumbles "Sorry, man" and slinks into his chair. Pablo gathers his books from the floor and looks around the room. His gaze stops briefly when he comes to Priti. I think he's as surprised as I am to see her here.

He takes in the rest of us and moves to the front of the room.

"Good morning, filmmakers!" he announces.

Noel is already raising his hand. What a shock. "Isn't it a little premature to call us filmmakers? I mean, aren't we here to learn how to be filmmakers?"

You have to hand it to Noel. He doesn't waste any time being both right and obnoxious.

Pablo shakes his head. "Actually, Noel, most of you already *are* filmmakers. You just don't realize it."

He reaches into his pocket and pulls out his phone. "How many of you have ever used this to record a video?"

Every hand goes up.

"That's different," Priti says in her low, authoritative voice. "A filmmaker does more than just record things in their lives."

"Yeah, she's totally right," Nathan yells from the back of the class. Priti turns and stares at him. He smiles back. I think he's trying to impress her.

I'm not all that good at reading expressions on people's faces (especially girls'), but Priti's is clearly saying "Who asked you?"

She turns back to Pablo.

"First off, there are filmmakers who *do* use events in their everyday lives to make their movies," Pablo says.

"Like vloggers!" RPG suggests.

Pablo nods. "Well, sure. But when you are taking videos or even selfies, are you *really* just pushing the button?"

He looks at me. I think for a second. "Well—"

Before I can finish my thought, Noel interrupts. "Usually I see something funny or cool happening and want to capture it so I can show it to my friends."

"Okay, Noel, let's hear from someone else."

How often does Noel hear this? Like, I mean how many times a day?

Pablo turns to me again. He checks his paper. "You're . . . Alex, right?"

Before Mateo or Nathan can chime in with any Xan-related humor, I nod. "Yes. Alex. That is my name."

RIP, Xan. He had a good run. Back to boring old Alex.

I see Pablo is waiting for me to continue. "So I guess . . . when we use our phones, we're *kind of* filmmakers, but isn't there more to it than just, like, deciding what to film?"

"If there wasn't, this would be a very short course!" Pablo says, laughing. He turns back to Priti. "You don't *really* just press the button, do you?"

Priti smiles. "I guess I don't. I mean, you have to decide what's a good background and what the best angle is, and even the lighting makes a difference to how good you look."

"You look good in *any* lighting," Jojo, one of the gymnastic triplets, says. "I've seen all your videos."

"Those are just the ones I post," Priti answers. "I have ones where I look like a zombie."

"So the only difference is the lighting and how you hold the camera?" Pablo asks.

"Hey! Watch this!" Mateo calls from the back. He's scrunching his face so it looks like he has three chins and holding his camera down below it. Then he stretches out his neck and holds his camera at a higher angle. "I look like two completely different people!"

Noel rolls his eyes. "Everybody knows that trick. It was a meme years ago."

"Even I know it," Pablo says, and we all laugh.

Somehow when he tries to talk like one of us, it isn't as cringey. Maybe because he's so young?

Pablo claps his hands together. "Okay, so we've already determined that where you put your camera and how you light your scene are important to how you tell your story."

"What story?" Nathan asks from the back. "All we're talking about are dumb video posts."

"Priti's posts are *not* dumb," Oona says with the kind of emotion I would usually associate with someone finding out their kitten just died.

Priti smiles at her. Oona practically glows.

"You have to get your mind away from the idea that movies are just one thing. Every time we take a picture or a video, we are telling a story, whether we mean to or not," Pablo says.

"But doesn't a story have to have a plot?" RPG asks. "Like when we play *Reign of Dragons*. If all we did was wander around, it would be pretty boring."

"Wow. *ROD* players. Cool," Pablo says. "I've been known to play that on occasion with my friends."

Noel and RPG trade a very pathetic high five. I notice that Cammi is looking down into his books.

Pablo turns to the rest of the class. "Not all stories have

plots. Or at least ones that we see right away. Some film-makers like to make movies that are messy and maybe the stories do wander, because that's more true to life. These are all great questions. As we get further along in the class, I'm going to show you examples of movies with traditional story structure and others that break the rules. Now, can anyone tell me what other elements can be used to make a scene different?"

I think for a second. "Sound!" I yell out.

Pablo turns to the whiteboard. "*Yes*. Good one, Alex. Are the sounds loud? Muffled? Far off? Think about how that affects how we feel about a scene."

I sit back and realize that Priti is looking right at me.

Like she is seeing me for the first time.

I wish I could say she leans in and whispers, "You are so cool! You totally look like your name should be Xan. Maybe we can hang out sometime."

But she just stares at me for a second and then turns back to Pablo.

Hey, it's a start.

CHAPTER 5

Ambush at Haddad's

"...And then he showed us this scene from the same movie twice."

"Uh-huh ... twice ...," my dad murmurs. I can tell he's not really paying attention because he's scanning the shopping list my mom gave him. This is a weekly ordeal where I go with my dad to get the groceries. My mom puts stuff on the list like "nuts" and my dad is supposed to know what kind.

Some people might think this means "pick out the nuts *you* like," but not with my mom. My dad did that once and she was all like, "Where are the cashews?"

Did my mom learn from that? No, she still writes these lists that are like mystery novels, with only clues to what the actual thing is that she wants. It drives my dad crazy.

Not only that, but because part of my mom's job is designing greeting cards, the lists are always written out in different fancy fonts, like calligraphy. Some of them are really pretty but hard to read.

We're in Haddad's and I can see the vein in my dad's head throbbing next to his glasses. He thrusts the list at me. "Your mother! Can you believe this? She writes 'olives.' Just 'olives.' *Really??*"

This is kind of funny because Haddad's is a gourmet store specializing in Middle Eastern foods, and one of their big specialties is that they have thirty-seven different kinds of olives.

My dad sighs and picks up his phone to call my mom. This is a ritual that has already been repeated many times throughout our trip:

"What *kind* of apples?" "Did you want *organic* or regular lettuce?" "Which *size* can of tomato paste?"

Sometimes I think my mom makes the list vague because she enjoys seeing my dad get so irritated. He's a pretty calm guy, so it is kind of funny to see him get so wound up about groceries.

"Yes, well, you wrote 'olives.' That doesn't help me. What kind? Uh-huh. Right. That's okay. I'll probably call you later."

He hangs up and turns to me. "She wants to make a tapenade. So we're supposed to ask what's the best olive for that."

"So why couldn't she just write that on the list?" I ask.

"Exactly!" my dad practically shouts.

By backing him up, there's a better than even chance

that I'll be able to get some malted milk balls from the candy section.

I know what I'm doing.

We head over to the area where there are olives of all kinds arranged in barrels. They all look the same to me.

There is a girl who looks about my age in an apron handing a plastic container of olives to another customer. She's the granddaughter of the owner, Sammy Haddad. We see her on weekends when she helps out at the shop.

"Hey there!" my dad says. "Is there someone here who can help us?"

The girl laughs. "I'm someone. What can I get you?"

She gives me a quick look.

I feel the need to say something.

So I do. Something stupid, of course.

"Do you know anything about olives?" I ask.

"Olives? No idea what you're talking about."

She looks down at the hundreds of olives arrayed in front of her. "Oh, you mean these green things? Are they olives? I had *no idea*," she says, totally without smiling.

Then she cracks up. "Yeah. I know something about olives."

"Do you know the best olives for tapenade?" my dad asks.

She thinks for a second.

Then we hear a familiar booming voice. "Mr. Mayor! No one told me you were here!"

Sammy Haddad rushes up and vigorously shakes my dad's hand.

The "Mr. Mayor" thing is his little joke. My dad is in city government, but he's only a deputy commissioner in the Department of Buildings. But Sammy (nobody calls him Mr. Haddad) thinks that my dad has a "bright future ahead of him" and will one day be the mayor of New York, so he says he wants to get used to saying it now.

"We were asking your granddaughter about olives," my dad says.

"Ah! Natalie! My little genius!" Sammy beams.

He turns to me. "And you're Alex, right?"

Sammy's kind of amazing in that he remembers *everybody*.

"What grade are you in?" Sammy asks.

"I just started seventh," I answer.

"So did I!" Natalie says. "Where do you go?"

I can feel my face go red. "Saint Anselm's. You?"

"PS One-Two-Six," she says with a little edge to her voice.

With Saint Anselm's being a private school, the public school kids all think we're a bunch of stuck-up rich kids.

My dad is always reminding me that a lot of smart kids go to public school and that we should be grateful for the opportunity to go to a private school but not to think it makes us so great.

He turns to Sammy and asks, "So . . . you're the perfect person to ask. What are the best olives for a tapenade?"

Sammy bows to his granddaughter. "Well. Natalie?"

"I was just going to tell them that they could use a mild-flavored olive like the ponentine, salt-brine cured and packed in vinegar," Natalie says, "but traditionally you'd go with a kalamata, a Greek black olive that is harvested fully ripe, because of its rich and fruity flavor."

Wow.

Like my dad says, there are definitely smart kids in public school.

Sammy beams. "She's a genius, this one."

"And very persuasive," my dad adds. "We'll take a large container of the kalamata, please."

As Natalie spoons the olives into a container, my dad turns to me. "I'm sorry. You were telling me about your film class."

"Yeah," I begin again. "Last class Pablo showed the same scene twice. Once it was just a girl on the phone with no music behind her. It was kind of boring. She was just chatting away. Then he showed the scene again, this time with ominous music, and all of a sudden it was tense and scary, like someone was about to jump out from behind the drapes and stab her or something. The only difference was the music."

"Wow. That sounds really cool."

I was expecting my dad to say something, but that was Natalie, who had just put the price label on our olives and was listening.

"So you get to watch movies in your school? Like for credit?" she asked.

"Yeah, it's an . . . okay class. On filmmaking." I tried to make it sound not so great.

Natalie wiped her hands on her apron. "Must be nice to have electives like that."

I knew what she was really saying. *Must be nice to go to a rich kid's school.*

My dad thanks her for her advice and heads in the direction of the candy section.

He lets me order the ultimate malted milk ball, which is my favorite, and we get some chocolate-covered peanuts for Violet or else she'll whine nonstop. I also get some red licorice, and we move to the checkout line.

"So you're okay with not taking that video game class?" my dad asks.

"Yeah, I guess so. I mean, Lexie is pretty obnoxious about rubbing it in my face, but what else is new?"

My dad laughs. "She never lets up, does she?" Then I see his face freeze.

I follow his gaze and see that Mrs. Tolliver is heading our way.

Her blond hair is pulled back and held in place by a pair of sunglasses perched on her head like a tiara. She's still in her white tennis clothes. She seems to be always either coming from or going to the fancy-schmancy tennis club in our neighborhood. I don't think I've ever seen her in anything but tennis clothes.

I think maybe she sleeps in them.

There is a smile plastered on her face as she kind of shrieks my dad's name. "*Bill!* I haven't seen you in *ages!*"

She kisses my dad on the cheek, and he only flinches a little. She looks over at me and shakes her head. "My goodness,

Alex! You've grown a *foot!*" She turns to my dad. "He's grown a *foot!*"

Needless to say, I have not grown a foot. Or an arm, or any other appendage. I am exactly the same height as I was at the beginning of the summer. But I guess this is her way of "being charming."

I remember my mom telling my dad she thought Margot Tolliver "had work done," which I thought meant like on her house but now I realize means plastic surgery. I mean, obviously, because her eyebrows are so raised she looks perpetually surprised.

"Good to see you, Margot," my dad says in a tone that means "I don't want to continue talking to you."

"How *is* Alison?" Margot presses on, oblivious. "We haven't had you people over in *an age*. We are long overdue."

My dad pushes the cart ahead, calling back. "Maybe in a couple of months . . . you know, after . . ."

"After? After what?" Margot says, and the room gets very cold.

Okay, someone did open the door to the freezer section right next to us to get some ravioli, but still, that wasn't what froze the smile on Mrs. Tolliver's face.

My dad sighs and waves his hand. "You know, Margot, Calvin's project is up for review and—"

"Oh! I wasn't even *thinking* about that."

Mrs. Tolliver was totally thinking of that. Her son Adam is in the sixth grade, and he has been talking for a year about this huge development his father is going to build over on Court Street. We all know about it. And now they need permission from the Building Commission.

And since my dad is deputy commissioner, he's kind of part of that decision.

Other people wouldn't be so careful about socializing with people who are going to come before their committee, but my dad is like that. He wouldn't talk to my uncle Richie when Richie was just trying to add a parking garage under the apartment building his company was working on, and Richie was just the architect.

Mrs. Tolliver puts a clawlike hand on my dad's forearm. "Well, I'm sure there isn't going to be any problems with that, so once it's all settled, we'll have you over—and the boys can play!"

For the record, her son is a jerk who thinks he's cool because his family has lots of money. And whose idea of fun is a punching contest? I can never win because if I really punched him hard, he'd cry and run to his parents.

Yeah, *that* kid.

My dad gently pulls himself from her grasp. "Looks like they're calling me at cashier four," he says, and I follow him away from Cruella de Tennis.

He's pretty quiet as he pays for our stuff. I know it's hard for him when someone we know through school has a project up for review. I just usually don't have to see it play out.

We step outside and almost bump into an older man in a

dusty old corduroy blazer. His wispy gray hair is sticking up and he hasn't shaved. He's handing out some sort of paper to everyone passing by. He thrusts one into my dad's hand.

It reads: *Meeting to stop Court Street Towers! Preserve Brooklyn Heights and stop overdevelopment!*

He looks hopefully at my dad. "You'll sign the petition, right? We can't let these losers destroy our neighborhood!" He actually uses a stronger word than *loser,* but I'm trying to be nice here.

My dad gives him a sorrowful shake of the head. "I'm afraid I can't."

The old man's expression changes. "You *can't*? You mean you won't!"

We turn and head for home. I can hear the old man cursing us out halfway down the block.

CHAPTER 6

The Stakes Are Raised

We are now three weeks into the class and so far we've done nothing but watch movies. Well, not whole movies. Just clips from them—and in some cases Pablo turns it off just as it's getting good.

Like today. We're watching a scene from a gangster movie called *Goodfellas* where the main guy (sorry, main *character*) is taking his girlfriend to a nightclub and they walk in the back and thread their way through all these tables and then they sit down.

That was pretty much all there was to it. Pablo asks us to point out things about the scene that we noticed.

"He's talking over it," Noel says without raising his hand as usual.

Pablo nods. "There's a voice-over, as we call it. What does that add?"

RPG is waving his hand excitedly. I make a mental bet he will mention *Reign of Dragons*.

"It adds another layer and deepens the scene," RPG says, the words tumbling out like the many-sided dice he always has somewhere on his desk. "It gives the scene context—"

"Great!" Pablo exclaims, but RPG isn't finished.

"—it reminds me of when I'm the Game Master in *ROG* and describing a scene—"

An audible groan comes from the side of the room where Mateo and Nathan are sitting.

RPG glares at them. "May I finish, please?"

"Sure, killer," Nathan says.

"The Notorious RPG," Mateo says, and the two of them crack up.

Pablo sighs. "I think I know where you're going, Ralph. But there's something more amazing about the scene. Anyone spot it?"

I know the answer, but I let these other clowns go first.

"It's from the lead characters' POV—or point of view," I add, turning to Priti as if to explain it to her.

She, of course, isn't even looking at me.

What else is new.

Pablo looks at me, eyebrows knit. "Yes . . . that is certainly an important part of the scene. That we follow our lead character. But I'm looking for something else."

What? He isn't even impressed that I remembered POV?

"It's done in one continuous shot, with no cuts," Priti says. Of course.

Pablo smiles. "*Yes*. This is one of the most famous shots in cinema, what's called a *tracking shot*. As the camera follows along with the actors. A full three minutes with no cuts. Lots of movies have imitated it."

He is about to show other scenes from movies that use this technique when there is a commotion at the door.

Pablo checks his watch. "Oh. I didn't realize how long we've been talking. I meant to tell you guys we have a special announcement. Mr. Beaverton's class is going to join us."

Pablo gestures, and a bunch of other seventh graders pile in, grabbing seats. I forgot there was another film class. A tall older man joins Pablo at the front of the room.

I've vaguely heard of Mr. Beaverton, because he's been the film teacher at Saint Anselm's for so long (he started the program in, like, the seventies or something ancient). But he just seemed to be one of those older teachers who other people get.

He has a high forehead and a totally gray beard that is trimmed close to his face. He wears glasses, but something about him makes you want to call them "spectacles." He is wearing a suit with (I'm totally serious) a vest and a tie. You don't see too many Saint Anselm's teachers who go all out like this guy. I am a little disappointed that he doesn't have bushy eyebrows. His are thinner and more transparent.

Mr. Beaverton claps his hands and the room goes silent.

Even Pablo looks scared of him.

"Good morning to Mr. Rosenstein's class," he says in this deep sonorous voice, like the actor who plays Sauron in the Lord of the Rings movies.

Actually, that's who he looks like. Christopher Lee.

"I assume Pablo has informed you of the Golden Reel Competition," he continues.

Pablo clears his throat. "Actually, I lost track of time, so I didn't get to it."

Mr. Beaverton gives a thin little smile. It isn't nice. It has a totally Snape-like vibe that I'm sure is creeping out our whole class.

"Yes, well, Mr. Rosenstein, you never were particularly good at budgeting your time," he intones. "I remember your student film was entered too late to be considered."

Pablo went to Saint Anselm's? He never mentioned it. And he took film from Mr. Beaverton?

Wild.

Mr. Beaverton sighs heavily. "I suppose it falls upon me to enlighten your class. The Golden Reel is an annual competition of student films. At the end of the semester, we have a festival with a guest judge, who awards the Golden Reel to the film that demonstrates the greatest potential and mastery of the medium."

"Wait! We're going to be *making* films?" Noel calls out.

Mr. Beaverton pauses.

For like a full minute.

He finally speaks. "I don't recall asking for questions."

"Yes, Noel, you all will be making films," Pablo says.

There is stifled excitement from our class. We would normally be whooping it up, but clearly Mr. Beaverton has established a No Whooping Zone in this classroom.

I don't get why he had to come and tell us this. Clearly he already told his students, all of whom are sitting here looking at us like "you guys are total losers who are stuck with Pablo while *we* have the greatest film teacher in the history of film teaching."

"Normally, I would have simply let Pablo inform you of this, but there is a change this year," Mr. Beaverton says.

"This year we're being sent to an island where we kill each other, and the winner is the last one standing," Nathan volunteers from the back of the room.

There are stifled giggles.

I mean, you have to admire his nerve, to try to break the tension with a little humor. Who doesn't like a good *Hunger Games* reference, right?

You know who doesn't?

Mr. Beaverton, obviously.

"Mr. Rosenstein, please control your class."

"Actually, I thought it was kind of funny," Pablo says, earning major points from all of us.

"Shall I continue?" Mr. Beaverton asks. "I think even you might find this interesting."

Pablo shrugs. It seems he takes this whole competition thing a lot less seriously than Mr. Beaverton.

"The reason I have gathered both classes is that seeing as this is the fiftieth anniversary of film at Saint Anselm's, we have not one but two judges, both distinguished alumni of the school *and* this class."

Even Pablo looks intrigued.

"First off, we have Hannah Krausz, Emmy Award–winning writer and actress of the acclaimed series *Girl Problems.*"

The girls are, not surprisingly, totally psyched to hear this. Even though this is a series about young women just out of college trying to make it in New York, most of them watch it.

I don't know too many boys who do.

"And joining her is Cody Fantano, director of *Mexican Standoff* and the current *Paperback Original.*"

Wait, what? Cody Fantano went to Saint Anselm's?

Unfortunately, I didn't just think this—I said it out loud.

Beaverton turns slowly and looks at me. "Yes, young man. Cody Fantano went to Saint Anselm's. If you'd been listening, you would have heard me refer to him as one of our distinguished alumni. You *do* know what the word *alumni* means, I hope?"

"Yes," I manage to get out.

"May I continue?" he asks me, bowing slightly.

"Yes."

"Very well," he says. "As in years past, the winner of the Golden Reel will go on to compete in the international student film festival in Toronto, which, I might add, has been won by Saint Anselm's students five out of the last seven years."

We are all silent now.

"But also," Mr. Beaverton continues, "our judges have generously added to the prize. The winning team will be given the opportunity to spend part of the summer, all expenses paid, observing on location the filming of Ms. Krausz's and Mr. Fantano's current projects."

He cocks his head. Then, in annoyance, adds, "You may *now* express your enthusiasm."

We clap and cheer, and I look over at Pablo.

For some reason he doesn't look all that thrilled about this.

CHAPTER 7

The Plot (But Definitely Not the Maple Syrup) Thickens

I have been an extremely good sport about Lexie and Brandon spending most lunches discussing how incredibly amazing video game class is and how it's too bad I'm missing out.

Rather than dumping the contents of my tray in either of their laps, I have been mature enough to pretend to be excited for them. I might have let something slip out along the lines of "Wow, you got a ball to bounce on the screen. Look out, Nintendo!"

But that was just a momentary lapse in my quest to be a better person than either of those jerks.

I *did not* mention that Brandon uses enough body spray to fumigate the entire gym.

In fairness, Lexie asked me in the past what we were doing in film class, but when I said "Watching clips from movies," she and Brandon exchanged glances like, "We are so glad we are making cool video games and not just watching boring old movies."

But this lunch is different. And not just because we're having what the lunchroom people refer to creatively as "breakfast for lunch," which is just a way for them to serves us rubbery scrambled eggs, greasy sausages, and limp French toast.

We put our trays down and I cut off all further conversation about video games by saying, "So I just found out we're going to be making our own movies."

Lexie totally ignores me and dips a finger in the teeny-tiny plastic container of what is labeled *Maple Syrup* and makes a face. "If this is maple syrup, I'm bigfoot. It's like pure corn syrup with gross flavoring added."

Brandon grabs it from her. "Hey, if you don't want it—"

"I didn't say that," Lexie says, swiping it back. "Just for that, I'm taking one of your sausages."

"Hey! Did you guys hear what I just said?" I ask with a hint of annoyance.

But only a hint.

I am a very mature person.

Brandon turns to Lexie. "Do you have the math homework?"

"Sure, I'll give it to you after— *Hey!* Quit it!"

I just threw a large clump of scrambled egg at Lexie. I decided I am not *that* mature.

Lexie wipes the greasy blob from her T-shirt. "You better hope that doesn't leave a stain, Alex. This is my favorite shirt."

"I thought it was your only shirt," I say, and immediately regret it.

Lexie turns red and forcefully jams her fork into a piece of French toast. I assume in her mind it's my forehead.

"I'm sorry, Lexie. That was a jerky thing to say," I admit.

Lexie takes a deep breath. "Yeah, well, maybe I deserved it. We heard Nathan and Mateo talking all about the film competition in Bio, so we already know about it."

"It was Lexie's idea to mess with you," Brandon adds helpfully, throwing her under the bus.

"Remind me never to be in a resistance army with you," Lexie grouses. "If we got captured, you'd give me up in a second."

Brandon shrugs. "Yeah, I probably would."

"It actually sounds amazing," Lexie says to me, and for once she sounds like she's sincere. "Do you know what you want your movie to be about?"

"We just found out about it this morning," I say, "but the competition part is what's so especially awesome. Imagine being able to go on the set of a Cody Fantano movie and watch it being made."

"I guess that wouldn't be so cool for Rafaella," Brandon says.

He's right. Rafaella diBono is in our grade and her mom is Greta Bloom, the actress who you've seen in a million movies.

"Have you been in a class with her?" Lexie asks. "Whenever

the conversation turns to 'What did you do on summer break or Christmas vacation, she'll act all bored about 'having to go to Paris *again* because Mom is shooting there' or something equally obnoxious. Alex, you have goo on your chin."

I wipe off the non-maple-maple-syrup with my napkin. "The only one who can top her is Priti. She's always coming back from some glamorous place where her family stays in five-star hotels and then she puts a thousand photos on Instagram."

"It's no wonder she has so many followers," Brandon adds. "They all leave comments telling her how amazing she is, and how beautiful her photos are, blah blah blah . . ."

I shake my head. "They are so obsessed with her. It's pathetic."

Lexie looks at the two of us. "Oh yeah. *They're* the ones who are pathetic."

"What?" I ask.

Lexie gets up with her tray. "For guys who aren't obsessed with Priti, you two sure talk about her a lot."

She stomps off.

Noel sidles up with his tray. His plate has a dozen sausages and three of those micro boxes of non-maple-syrup. "This seat taken?"

"Nah, go ahead," I say. "Wow. How'd you get all that?"

"The lunch guys like me," he says, stuffing four sausages into his mouth at once.

"It would appear so," Brandon says. "So you're all making movies now?"

Noel nods, takes a swig of milk, and swallows. "Yeah, but it's not going to matter."

"What's not going to matter?" I ask.

"I mean, none of us are going to win the competition," Noel says in his usual way of suggesting that he has the inside scoop.

I hate to give him the satisfaction, but I need to know what he knows. "And how are you so sure of that?"

Noel grins. "I know everything."

"Just tell me, Noel."

"Okay, so here's the deal," Noel says. "Beaverton runs the thing. Both the judges were his old students. Not only that, but in the fifty years of the Golden Reel, one of Beaverton's students *always* wins. I looked it up. It doesn't matter who the other teacher is."

"Yeah, but what if one of us makes a better movie than one of Beaverton's students?"

Noel shakes his head. "Do you really think the best film is going to win? Grow up."

Having inhaled his lunch, Noel takes his tray and heads for the exit.

Well, that was kind of depressing to hear. Maybe that's why Pablo looked so bummed.

He knew his kids were never going to win.

Just as I think things can't get any worse, I see Felix Terrier-Borowitz heading in my direction.

"Hey! Alex! I wanna talk to you!"

Felix is our grade's radical. He is always boycotting

something and going to marches. Not that you shouldn't march for things you believe in. I went with my parents to the Black Lives Matter marches and it was really great.

I mean, it's cool he's so passionate and everything, but what he's *passionate* about seems to change every few months. And then he gets all superior about how none of us are as committed to whatever cause he's into right now.

"What's up?" I ask in as nonconfrontational a way as I possibly can.

Felix's face is as red as the hairs sticking up in all directions from his head. "You know what's up, Alex Davis. So your dad is going to vote against the Court Street project, right?"

"How the heck do I know?" I ask.

"He *better* vote against it. Our neighborhood is overbuilt as it is. And it means tearing down existing buildings, throwing old people onto the street. Is your dad in favor of that?"

"Yeah, my dad wants to throw old people onto the street," I shoot back. "Felix, please."

Felix pushes some papers into my hands. "This is a petition signed by half the kids in the seventh grade. Give it to him. He should know how we feel."

I sigh and accept the papers. "Okay, Felix, I can do that."

"I just hope your dad does the right thing," Felix says. "Otherwise, he should be ashamed of himself. Letting so many big buildings go up around here."

"He's just one vote," I remind him.

Felix crosses his arms. "I bet he could persuade the others, if he wasn't so busy having free meals with big developers."

"What are you talking about?" I practically shout.

"I know for a fact your family has had dinners with the Tollivers," he says triumphantly. "Who knows what was discussed there?"

"That was like two years ago. We never see them. And anyway, that's a terrible thing to say about my dad."

"Fine," Felix says. "I hope I'm wrong. But give him this."

I look at the petition. It says:

We, the undersigned, demand that no more high-rise apartment complexes be built in our neighborhood, pushing up rent prices and creating more garbage and congestion in our streets. We want to inherit a world with less waste, not more.

Stop the march of greed and corruption now! Stop the developers!

I scan the list of signatures. Felix has definitely been busy. There must be close to fifty or so kids who signed.

On the first line, I see, in black magic marker, *Lexie Mizell.*

CHAPTER 8

Winners and Losers

The classroom is buzzing when I get there. Clearly, Noel spread the word about what he learned.

As usual, Pablo is late and wanders in, coffee mug in one hand and laptop in the other. As soon as he sits down behind his desk, kids begin calling out questions, or in Nathan's and Mateo's case, just yelling, "Pablo! *Hey!*"

Pablo looks confused and raises his hands to quiet us down. "Okay, so what's got you all riled up like this? I mean, I know Mr. Beaverton can be a little heavy, but—"

Jojo raises her hand straight up. "It's not about him, exactly."

Pablo turns to her. "Okay, so what's up?"

Jojo looks around, trying to figure out the best way to ask

about the Golden Reel. "Well . . . we heard . . . that like for the past fifty years, kids from Mr. Beaverton's class always win the prize."

Pablo's head drops. He closes his eyes. "Yes, that's right. So what?"

Noel lets out a groan of exasperation. "So, it's fixed."

Pablo lifts his mug of coffee. He takes a long sip. "What if it is?"

Oona groans. "Then what's the point?"

Pablo slams his mug so hard on the desk I'm shocked it doesn't break. "What's the point? What's the *point*?"

Oona realizes she's said exactly, totally the wrong thing and mumbles, "I mean, I know we're not here to win contests and everything, but . . ."

"I don't expect you to get this right now, but I'm going to say it anyway," Pablo says. "The worst thing you can do is create something just to please someone else. It will kill your soul. It will take something that is one of the most beautiful things you can do in this sad old world and ruin it. I know."

There is silence as we all take this in.

"I really wanted you to have an *experience* in this class. To learn to tell *your* stories the way you want to. There will be plenty of time to make art for other people. This is for you. But Mr. Beaverton runs the department, so I had to let him come in and talk to you."

Priti speaks up, slowly. "Does . . . this mean you don't want us to submit our films to the Golden Reel?"

Pablo turns to her. "No. Of course you should have your

films seen by two of our most successful alumni in the business."

"Maybe you just don't think we're as good as the kids in Mr. Beaverton's class," Noel says, as usual going to exactly the wrong place.

Pablo looks at his coffee mug for a long time. I never noticed, but the design is actually a logo from a movie studio, the one with the roaring lion in it.

"Noel, I have a feeling this is the most talented group of kids I have ever taught." This inspires high fives between Nathan and Mateo, who are definitely not the kids he's talking about.

"But you haven't even seen anything we've filmed," Priti says.

"It's the way you talk about the clips I show—the things you see in them. And I *have* seen things you've done. Your social media feed, for example. The way you compose your shots. You have a real eye. And the way RPG, Noel, and Cammi show great narrative ability already in composing stories with actual arcs and an intuitive grasp of structure."

Jojo's hand shoots up. "So you're saying we could be the first non-Beaverton class to win the Golden Reel?"

There is a flurry as we all clap and whoop for one another and our collective awesomeness.

"No!" Pablo almost yells. "I'm saying I couldn't give a— I don't care if you win or not. The one thing I want you to take away from this class is that winning is *not* why you make art. What is winning, anyway? I mean, it's just someone's opinion."

"Excuse me," Joie says, her eyes blazing. "Some of us care very much about winning. When I got a gold medal for my vault in the junior meet last year and helped our team with the overalls, it felt amazing. You're telling me that's nothing?"

"She was awesome. And millions of people root for their sports teams like it's the most important thing in the world. So you're just saying they're all stupid?" Jojo demands.

"No!" Pablo says. "I just mean—"

"That's just loser talk," Nathan says, smiling at Joie. "He's just sore 'cause that Beaverton guy kicks his butt every year."

I've been quiet this whole time, but I feel I need to say something. Pablo looks deflated.

"Guys, I think I know what Pablo is talking about."

"Words of wisdom from another loser," Mateo says.

Thanks, Mateo.

"It's just that . . . who wins is subjective. You know? Like even in some sports. Aren't there judges who decide to give you a score based on their opinion of how well you did?"

Oona bites her lip. "Yeah, I guess that's true."

I press on. "I know in the Olympics there's always some scandal about the judges awarding a medal to someone because they're biased, right?"

Noel nods. "Like that skater last year. My sister didn't stop crying for a whole day, and my dad kept trying to explain to her that just because her favorite got the silver medal doesn't make her any less incredible."

"That's why I like *Reign of Dragons*!" RPG exclaims right

on cue. "There are no winners or losers." He turns to Cammi, who quietly adds, "We all work together as a team to defeat the enemy."

"So if we work together, we're going to defeat the enemy, Mr. Beaverton's class?" Nathan asks.

"Just forget Mr. Beaverton's class!" Pablo pleads. "Just make the best little films that you can!"

He scans the room and sees Priti's hand is up. He nods to her.

"So . . . is that why you handed in your film so late?" she asks. "Because you didn't want to compete?"

Pablo gives her a small smile. "I wish. No, when I was your age, and even older, I wanted more than anything to win that Golden Reel. I just got so wrapped up in making my film perfect, I missed the deadline."

"So you blew your chance," Noel says.

"Not totally," Pablo says. "What Mr. Beaverton forgot to mention was that it was entered in the international film festival anyway, by the other film teacher, Ms. Dobksi. She thought it was good enough, I guess."

"So what happened?" RPG asks.

"It's not important," Pablo says. And turns to his computer.

We all know that's what someone says when they lose.

"What year was that?" Nathan asks.

"Um . . . let's see . . . 2002, I guess," Pablo answers.

Mateo looks down at his phone. "Hey, check this out! So your film was called *Pig Latin*?"

Pablo nods and busies himself with something at his desk.

Nathan holds up his phone like a trophy. "Not important, huh? It only won *first prize*!"

We all jump out of our seats and gather around Nathan's phone, except Priti, who sits, looking at Pablo.

"Are you ashamed of winning?" she asks.

Pablo looks up and addresses the class. "It's not that I'm ashamed. It's just that it messed me up for years. I kept trying to please everyone else. They all wanted me to repeat what I'd done with *Pig Latin* and I wanted to move on."

"I would've just given them what they wanted," Nathan says. "Hey, once you make enough money, you can do what you want, right?"

"It doesn't work that way, at least not for me," Pablo says. "I needed to do what made me happy. Otherwise, why do it? You're just a sellout."

"My parents make films for the money," RPG says. "They make ads and corporate films. Are they sellouts?"

Pablo puts his head in his hands. "Of course not, Ralph. I mean, if that's what feeds their soul, good for them."

"It feeds their kids," Ralph mutters.

Pretty much the whole class is standing around Pablo's desk. He pushes up from his chair and walks to the window.

He doesn't turn as he speaks to us.

"You know what? Go for it. Make films you think will beat Beaverton's class. Try and please some judges you don't even know. Don't mind me."

Cammi speaks up. "No. We want to make films that make you proud of us."

Pablo starts to say something. Then he stops himself. It looks like he's wiping his eyes, but maybe he's just cleaning his glasses.

Finally, he turns back to us.

"Just do the films you want to do. Just make good films. And who knows? Maybe one of them *will* win."

We look at each other, grinning. Then I catch a glimpse of Pablo's coffee mug, with the movie logo on it. It says MGM and underneath is a Latin phrase.

"Hey, Pablo, what does *ars gratia artis* mean?"

Priti, to no one's surprise, knows Latin.

"Art for art's sake," she says.

CHAPTER 9

Lexie and I Visit
a Local Landmark

"I think Pablo's right," Lexie says, scanning the vast selection of candy in front of her.

We are in Harry's, a little grocery and candy store that is what people think of when they say that development is running all the small businesses out of Brooklyn. It's a tiny little place, but all us kids from Saint Anselm's love it because Joe, the guy behind the counter, makes it a point to know all our names, and Donte, his buddy who makes all the sandwiches, somehow remembers every one of our orders.

"Hey, Alex, bagel and cream cheese toasted light?" Donte calls out as I stand next to Lexie.

"Not today, thanks," I answer.

Someone clears their throat behind us. I turn and see an

older woman glaring at us. She's clearly here for her daily lottery tickets, but the store is so narrow she can't get past us to the cash register.

We squeeze over to let her pass, and she grumbles something under her breath about *kids these days,* which is a phrase that's probably been said in Harry's for like a hundred years or more.

"Hi, Eileen," Joe calls out cheerfully. "You got your numbers?"

Eileen pulls a grimy wad of paper from her pocket and reads off a series of numbers. For the life of me, I can't figure out how the lotto thing works, but I guess it does because Eileen wins five dollars and her whole face lights up. You would have thought she'd won that 250-million-dollar grand prize that's marked on the sign (no one's won it in months) the way she's carrying on.

"I dunno about that," I say to Lexie, pointing to Eileen. "Everybody loves a winner."

"But that's different," Lexie says. "That's just dumb luck."

Eileen gives her a stare that could kill a charging rhino, but Lexie is oblivious. She's still weighing her candy options.

"Just get the peanut M&M's," I groan, "like you always do."

Joe looks over and smiles at Lexie. "Not always. Sometimes Lexie gets Twizzlers."

Lexie looks down shyly. "See? Joe knows." She grabs the Twizzlers, which she totally wouldn't have done if he hadn't said that.

I shake my head. "Whatever. I just think you're jealous because there isn't a competition in your video games class."

Lexie looks at me like I've grown another head. "Nuh-uh. You know I hate competing for things. Except *playing* video games," she adds before I can laugh in her face.

We've reached the counter, and Lexie pays for her Twizzlers and I get some gum.

The door swings open and some tourists poke their heads in. I know they're tourists because they are taking pictures of everything in the store and the wife is wearing an I ♥ NY T-shirt, which no real New Yorker would be caught dead in.

The husband has a Chicago Cubs baseball cap on and he turns to Joe. "Excuse me, would you know where we could find a good Chinese restaurant around here?"

I cringe and see Lexie bite her lip. Her mom's family came here from Mexico years ago and they still get asked by parents at our school, no less, where to get "real Mexican food." Jeez.

I mean, Joe's not even Chinese. He's Korean. But of course he doesn't say that. He just nods and says, "If you go up two blocks to Montague Street, there's a whole bunch up there."

The man grins. "I told her you'd know."

Oh, *man*.

His wife pushes past us and yells at her husband, "I'm getting water. You want one?"

"You can grab me a beer!" He guffaws and winks at me. Like he couldn't get any grosser.

Lexie and I wave goodbye to Joe and Donte, who call out "Bye, Lexie! Bye, Alex!" like they always do when we leave.

By this time, more kids are piling into the store to get after-school snacks. Not just kids from Saint Anselm's either.

As we head up the three little steps leading to the street, a group who looks about our age darts past us, laughing and pushing each other.

There is a flash of black hair and I realize that one of the girls is the one from Haddad's. Sammy's granddaughter. She catches my eye and her expression changes. She gives me a little nod and goes into the store.

Lexie doesn't miss anything. "Who's that girl? She acted like she knows you."

"She's Sammy Haddad's granddaughter," I say. "She was helping out at their shop the last time my dad and I were there."

"I thought she looked familiar," Lexie says, tearing open her Twizzlers and taking a huge bite.

The light changes and we walk down the street toward our houses.

"Maybe I should do a film about Haddad's," I think out loud.

"That would be cool," Lexie says. "But what would be the story?"

The story? "I haven't thought that far ahead," I snap at her.

"You have to have a story," Lexie says, suddenly the expert filmmaker.

"Okay, like what kind of story?" I ask.

"I dunno . . . *Hey!*" Lexie turns to me. "I got it. A ghost story! Kids love ghost stories."

"A ghost story set in Brooklyn Heights?" I laugh. "I don't think so."

"Fine," Lexie says, putting the last Twizzler in her mouth (that girl eats *fast*).

Instead of turning down our street, Lexie continues down Joralemon Street toward the water.

"Aren't you going home?" I ask.

Lexie nods in the direction of Brooklyn Bridge Park. "Come on, there's someone I want you to meet."

Huh. This seems weird. "Who is it?"

"It's hard to explain," Lexie says, heading downhill.

I follow her. Lexie looks at the beautiful buildings on either side of us, none taller than six stories.

"I love this area, don't you?" She sighs.

I have to admit it's pretty cool. Once you pass Hicks Street, the road turns into cobblestones, as if you were walking into the past.

"I can almost imagine horse-drawn carriages passing through here, can't you?" Lexie asks.

I scrunch up my nose. "Think of all that horse poop. It must have smelled pretty rank."

The next street takes us under the expressway. This is the big highway that takes all the cars and trucks heading from other parts of Brooklyn into Manhattan and back.

Lexie looks up. "Did you know that the expressway was supposed to go right through the center of the Heights?"

"Of course I do," I say. "We had history with Ms. Chan together."

"Didn't you do your paper on how we were the first neighborhood to get historical landmark designation?"

I nod, impressed that Lexie remembers. "Yeah, everyone banded together to stop the developers from ruining the character of the . . ."

My voice trails off. I see where this is going.

Lexie looks smug but doesn't say anything.

We've reached the park, which is right on the water, overlooking the skyline of Manhattan. Lexie points to our left and then to our right. Large apartment towers loom over the area, cold and metallic.

"See? How would you like to live in a Brooklyn Heights filled with buildings like that?" she asks.

Now she's on my turf. My dad's commission approved each of these buildings. "Lexie, you enjoy the park, right? It's pretty awesome, and people from all over Brooklyn can enjoy it."

"Yeah, so?" Lexie says.

"So, how was all this paid for? The city doesn't have the money. All these big buildings paid for it. And continue to pay for it. In taxes."

Lexie holds up her hand. "Okay. So you're saying there's a trade-off?"

"In this case, yeah, sure," I answer.

Lexie has brought me to the area where there are small coffee shops, bakeries, and other places for the people who live all the way down here to shop. There are tables set up under the trees. Lexie brings me over to one of the tables, where two older men are playing chess.

One is dressed in a tracksuit, with sunglasses and a gold chain. His white hair is combed neatly back and he has a small cup of espresso next to him.

I look at the other man, in his rumpled jacket and hair sticking out in all directions. Under his seat is a shopping bag with a clipboard and sheafs of paper.

Petitions. It's the same crazy old guy from outside Haddad's. *Wonderful.*

Lexie clears her throat.

Without looking up, the petition guy waves his hand in our general direction. "One moment, sweetheart. I'm about to beat Mr. Birnbaum here."

Mr. Birnbaum chuckles and crosses his arms across his gut. I am suddenly aware that Mr. Birnbaum might be the only human to wear more cologne than Brandon. "Dream on, Harvey."

Petition Man sighs and looks up at Lexie. His face breaks out in a smile. It's the first time I've seen him not look angry.

"It's you! So nice of you to stop and say hello!" he says.

Lexie indicates me. "Mr. Konigsberg, this is my friend Alex."

The two men exchange glances. "Your *friend*?" Mr. Birnbaum asks, grinning.

"We're just friends!" Lexie and I blurt out in unison.

Old people, they can be so annoying at times.

"Mr. Konigsberg and I met when I signed his petition," Lexie explains.

Mr. Konigsberg looks proud. "She wasn't going to do it, until I told her my story."

Okay, so now I'm hooked. "Your story?"

Mr. Konigsberg looks over at Mr. Birnbaum, who takes a sip of his espresso and leans back. Clearly, this is quite a story.

"So, how long do you think I've been living in Brooklyn, young man?" he asks.

I shrug. "I dunno, maybe fifty years?"

Mr. Konigsberg holds up a finger, like a king making a royal decree. "Since 1938, I'll have you know. Born and raised. I've lived through a lot, let me tell you."

"He's going to tell you, believe me," mutters Mr. Birnbaum.

Mr. Konigsberg ignores his friend. "I mean, through good times and bad, Harvey Konigsberg has been here. I've lived on Atlantic Avenue, in the same apartment, going about my business, and then spending the rest of my life happily in retirement beating this gentleman here at chess."

"That remains to be seen," Mr. Birnbaum says evenly.

Mr. Konigsberg's face hardens. "Until that letter arrived. That—"

"Careful, there are young people here," Mr. Birnbaum warns.

"That, er . . . *dumb* letter from Hewitt Properties."

"What letter?" I ask.

Mr. Konigsberg turns to me. "I'm getting to that. Don't be so impatient."

"Go on, Mr. Konigsberg," Lexie says.

Mr. Konigsberg smiles at Lexie. "A sweetheart, this one. So where was I? Oh, yes, the letter. It told me my building was sold. Sold out from under me. Throwing me out on the street like a cockroach."

I can feel Lexie looking at me.

"So they could build that lousy monstrosity."

He gestures vaguely behind him.

Lexie whispers to me, "You know that apartment complex that went up on Atlantic and Hicks?"

I do remember it. My dad doesn't talk a lot about his work, but this one was in the papers. Hewitt Properties had promised the buildings commission they would use first-class materials, and then after getting approvals, Hugh Hewitt ended up using the cheapest grade of cement, the flimsiest walls, bad wiring. There were lots of lawsuits.

"But that was just one building," I protest. "And Hugh Hewitt isn't even involved in this building."

"Ah, they're all alike," Mr. Konigsberg grumbles. "A bunch of crooks."

I'm about to say something when Lexie stops me.

"So tell Alex what happened next," she says gently.

"What's to tell?" Mr. Konigsberg asks. "I was a renter. He broke my lease and I ended up on the street, like a dog, like a—"

"Enough about the cockroaches already," Mr. Birnbaum

says. "You're not on the street." He looks at me. "My wife died a few years ago. My kids live on their own. Meet my new roommate."

"He lives with you?" I ask.

Mr. Birnbaum adjusts his tracksuit and his chain jingles. "Why not? It beats talking to the TV."

Mr. Konigsberg has turned his attention back to the chessboard. "Whose move was it anyway?"

Mr. Birnbaum shrugs. "Who remembers?"

We say our goodbyes and turn to head home.

"Now you know why I signed the petition," Lexie says.

"Yeah, okay, but—"

"By the way, you two make a lovely couple!" Mr. Birnbaum yells after us, chuckling.

We race across the street.

Lexie's face is bright red. "I can't *believe* he said that!"

"I know, right?" I answer, feeling the heat in my own cheeks.

For a second (but *just* a second), I allow myself to think of what it would be like to be a "lovely couple" with Lexie.

I guess Lexie catches the expression on my face. "It's so *gross*."

"Totally," I agree.

We don't say another word until we split up and go to our respective houses.

CHAPTER 10

The Unknown Advantages of Skate Camp, and ... Who the Heck Is Theo?

The next day in film class, I slide into my seat, which I've occupied for the first three weeks of school.

I realize with a start that Pablo is already at his desk. This is a first since he always comes in ten minutes late. He looks like he's really psyched.

The bell rings, and he claps his hands and everyone turns to him.

"Okay," Pablo begins. "So this is going to be a little bit of a surprise for some of you. When Mr. Beaverton told you we would be making movies, what he didn't mention was that you guys are going to be working in teams."

There is a not-so-muted "Yes!" from RPG and Noel.

I raise my hand. "Um . . . is there a reason we can't make our own film?"

Pablo takes a sip of coffee. "Well, I suppose you *could* make your own film. That usually happens in the third year. Do you know how to record sound? Are you planning to hold the boom mic *and* operate the camera at the same time?"

I feel my face getting hot. "I . . . guess I hadn't thought about that part."

"Yeah," Pablo says. "Most kids don't appreciate everything that goes into making a movie until they do it themselves. Believe me, you'll thank me."

Pablo unbuckles his briefcase (of course his briefcase has buckles) and pulls out a piece of paper.

"I have made up a list of the teams for this year's projects," he reads.

I look around the room and realize that most likely I will be put with Nathan and Mateo. I mean, who else would it be?

"Team one will be Oona, Jojo, and Joie."

Gosh, who would have seen that coming?

"Team two is Ralph, Noel, and Cammi."

Yeah, that makes sense.

Here it comes . . .

"Team three is going to be a two-man team—Nathan and Mateo."

Wait. *What?*

"And team four will be Alex, Priti, and Theo."

Pablo puts the sheet back in his briefcase. "I will give you the rest of the class to discuss your possible projects."

Okay, first of all . . . I'm making a film with Priti?

Second, who the heck is *Theo*?

I turn to Priti to see how ticked off she is to be working with me instead of Oona, Joie, and Jojo, who are currently whispering to each other and pointing in my general direction. I definitely do *not* want to know what they're saying.

But if she's mad, I wouldn't know it. I gingerly slide over to the chair next to hers and I hear myself chattering away, "I'msosorryI'msureyouwouldhavepreferredtoworkwiththegirlswecantalktoPablo—"

Priti looks directly into my eyes, which is disconcerting enough, but then she comes out with this: "Don't be silly, Alex. I *asked* to work with you."

You know those pictures that are all over the Internet, where it looks like one thing (like a person with three legs, or something more embarrassing) and then you look closer and realize that it's an illusion, or a trick your eyes have played on you? That's how I feel when Priti says that she asked to be on my team.

I am very proud of myself for *not* saying something totally dumb like "You want to work with *me*? Why?"

Instead I say something far more cool and sophisticated: "Huh?"

Priti cocks her head to one side and smiles. "Alex, I saw

the videos you posted from skate camp. You are an amazing editor. And a lot of those shots were really cool. The way you matched them up with the music was excellent too."

I am still processing the fact that Priti keeps saying my name. "Yeah . . . I mean, thanks. I really like the stuff you post too."

Yikes. Now she'll think I'm stalking her.

But why was she on *my* feed?

"Oh, cool! So you were like me," Priti says. "Checking out everyone in our class to see who the good filmmakers are."

"Yeah, that's right," I say, totally forgetting to mention I had no intention of taking Film Studies.

"So glad Pablo put us together," Priti says, and I get this tingling feeling when she smiles at me.

No, not *that*. I mean, we've all taken health class. It's . . . different. It's like she's really *seeing* me. Which is ridiculous. But also undeniable.

Speaking of being seen, I suddenly realize that we're not alone. I turn and practically jump out of my skin when I realize someone has been sitting next to me the entire time.

I can't believe how quietly he slipped into the seat.

I swear I have never seen him in class before.

And it's not like he would be easy to overlook.

He has shoulder-length black hair, a tight-fitting black turtleneck shirt, and black sweatpants that graze his ankles. And some kind of sandals with black socks. His face is so pale and narrow it's almost creepy. Like he's wearing makeup or something.

I guess you could sum up the look as "renegade mime."

Priti gives him a dazzling smile and says, "You must be Theo. I don't think we've met."

Theo nods. "You're Priti Sharma. Your father is a partner in Dhanpati Capital Investments. And your mom is on the board of United Way and the New Museum." He turns to me. "And your father is deputy buildings commissioner, and your mom is a freelance graphic artist."

"Okay," I say, "glad to meet you. Why do you know about our parents?"

Theo shrugs. "I like to know things. Like I knew that we were going to be put together."

"You mean you guessed," Priti says.

Theo is impassive. "I never guess. I gather information."

Okay. So I'm starting to move Theo from the "charmingly eccentric" column into the "creeper vibes" column.

"Cool," Priti says, extending her hand. "Welcome to the team."

Theo regards her outstretched hand with distaste. "I don't shake hands. Unsanitary."

Priti nods. "That's cool too. So I take it you've just joined the class."

Theo smirks. "I've been in the back of the classroom this entire time."

That smirk.

It's an expression I'm going to get sick of really quickly.

In fact, I already have.

"I don't remember you back there. Why hasn't Pablo called on you?" I ask.

"That's between Pablo and me," Theo says. "And you didn't notice me because you've been staring at Priti here nonstop since the first day."

"That is totally not true!" I say a little too loudly.

It is totally true, but how did he know? And the way he says *Pablo,* it sounds like they're best friends.

Priti clearly believes Theo can be spoken to like a normal kid. "But you *are* new this year. I mean, you haven't been hiding since first grade."

A smile appears on the horizon of Theo's mouth, but he covers it with a hand.

A rubber-gloved hand.

He notices me staring at his hands. "Germs," he explains. "Also, fingerprints."

Pablo has been moving from group to group and joins ours.

"So you guys are getting acquainted?" he asks.

"I guess so," I say. "We were just about to ask Theo where he came from."

Theo swivels his head and stares directly at me. Then turns to Pablo. "I don't really want to talk about it."

Pablo nods. "That's cool, Theo. We're not here to pry into your life. We're here to make movies. Right, gang?"

Yikes. He called us "gang." Theo has thrown Pablo so far

off his game he's talking like a cheesy grown-up. If he calls us "kiddos" next, then all hope is lost.

"Right," Priti says, taking out a binder. Wouldn't you know it, she's already labeled it *Untitled Film Project*.

She opens it and smooths out the first page, turning to us. "So, any ideas? Make them good. I mean, we are going to win the Golden Reel after all."

Theo laughs. "What's the point? We all know someone from that jerk Beaverton's class is going to win."

"You don't know that," Priti says with surprising passion. "We just need to make the best film."

"Even if we made the most amazing film in the history of Saint Anselm's, you know Beaverton's old students are going to vote for his students," I insist.

Theo has been looking at his phone.

I have to go on about this phone for a minute. It's not a regular phone, but something in a huge black case made of some material that looks like it could stop bullets. He enters a code and then holds it up to his eyes.

"Facial recognition and iris scan," he informs us.

Priti is finally not having it. "So we're supposed to be impressed? My phone has biometrics too. Most of ours do."

"Yeah, but mine is set to wipe the phone of all data if anyone else so much as looks at the screen," Theo says.

"Dude, we're not going to look at your phone," I promise.

Theo smiles. It's not like an "I'm happy" smile. More like an "Aha!" smile.

"Now I see why you're so confident," he says to Priti. "DCI

invested in one of Cody Fantano's movies." He turns to me. "DCI stands for—"

"Dhanpati Capital Investments," I say with annoyance. "I figured that out all by myself."

Priti's eyes are flashing. "I had no idea about that. I mean, I know my dad's company invests in a lot of things, but he never talks about it."

"Sure, okay, I believe you," Theo says, meaning exactly the opposite.

I step in. "Look, you guys, we've got to find a way to work together. I don't care about winning prizes. I like what Pablo said."

Both Priti and Theo are silent for a moment.

I decide to call Theo's bluff. I grab his phone. "Listen, if you don't start behaving like we're a team, I'm going to look into the screen and wipe your phone."

If possible, Theo turns even paler than before. "Give me my phone back. Now."

I throw it to him, and he grabs for it. It clatters to the floor, where it bounces.

Theo reaches down, picks up his phone, and cradles it. "Don't ever do that again. I'm serious."

"Fine," I say. "Chill out. *Seriously.*"

I look around the room. I see the Gymnast Girls excitedly writing down ideas and hugging.

There's a guffaw from the corner, and I see Nathan falling on the floor like he hit his head on something and Mateo is saying, "That's *perfect*!" I'm guessing any movie ideas they're thinking of aren't going to be about ending world hunger or climate change.

RPG has taken some huge book from his backpack with the words *Reign of Dragons: Game Master's Manual* that he and Noel and Cammi are poring over.

We're the only team who hasn't come up with *anything*.

CHAPTER 11

Miserable and Snitty

It is lunchtime and we are having gyros, which are actually not as bad as the other meat products we have to suffer through.

It's still not exactly "meltingly tender," which is how it is described on the menu. It definitely needs some work to get the gyro down.

Lexie has just taken a bite of her pita and is chewing, which gives me a chance to actually get out more than one sentence.

"I'm telling you it was weird. I am willing to swear on a stack of *Video Games Insider* magazines that he has *not* been in that class before today."

Lexie gulps some water to push the gyro down. "You were probably too busy staring at Priti to notice."

"That's what he said!" I say. "And it's totally—"

"Wait! Did I just miss a joke?" Brandon joins us. Normally I would have smelled the body spray a good five minutes before he showed up, but the gyros are made with a *lot* of garlic at Saint Anselm's.

"What are you talking about?" Lexie asks.

"I just heard Alex say 'that's what he said,' so I assumed it was a punchline, you know, like—"

"We know," I quickly respond. Brandon is a little behind the curve on the humor front, and so has only recently discovered the joys of "That's what she said."

Lexie ignores all this and scoots over to make room for Brandon. "Alex is going to be working on his film with Priti Sharma and one of the new kids."

Brandon chokes on his pita. "*What?* You and Priti Sharma? How much did you bribe Rosenstein to get that to work out?"

"Actually, she chose *me,*" I say about as casually as one would say "Actually, there is a tarantula crawling on your face."

Lexie slaps Brandon on the back, hard. A lot harder than she needed to. "It seems Priti saw Alex's skateboard videos he posted this summer and was super impressed. She's better than me. I watched one and figured I had better things to do."

"Way to be supportive, Lexie," I say. "At least she appreciates what I was trying to convey."

Lexie leans past Brandon and grabs a pita from my plate.

"Yeah, like you were so supportive when I was in the play last year. You wouldn't help me learn my lines once."

"You had three lines!" I protested. "Wait! I even remember one of them! 'Look there! Under the bushes!'"

Lexie narrows her eyes. "It was 'Hark, comrades! Under yon bushy tree!' See, I knew you weren't paying attention."

"I got the basic gist of it," I say. "Your gyro is getting cold."

Priti comes up to us and puts her tray down.

At *our* table.

Priti Sharma.

"It's pronounced *hee*-ro," she says, wiping her silverware with her napkin.

Lexie rubs her nose. "We pronounce it *jy*-ro."

"The proper Greek pronunciation is *hee-ro*," Priti says evenly.

"Yeah, well, we're in New York, and not all of us have been to Greece," Lexie answers, "and here we say jy-ro."

Okay, I have to give what Pablo would call the backstory on why Lexie and Priti are this way with each other.

From first grade to fourth grade, Lexie's best friend was Isabel Archer. They were like inseparable, dressing the same and going to each other's houses after school.

Then Priti came to Saint Anselm's in fourth grade and middle-school drama ensued, with Isabel suddenly hanging out with Priti more and more, and even dressing like her, in polo shirts and chino pants, which understandably did not sit well with Lexie.

She got really mad and wrote a story about two girls who

sounded an awful lot like Isabel and Priti who are mean to this other girl and ultimately are turned into flesh-eating zombies who meet a gruesome death at the hands of an avenging angel.

I thought Lexie would get in trouble for stealing the plot of her story from a manga comic book series she and I had read together that summer, but people seemed more upset about her writing mean things about her classmates. She swore it wasn't about them, but *ahem,* she named the characters Miserable and Snitty, which sounds an awful lot like Isabel and Priti, don't you think?

Well, our English teacher, Mr. Sakurai, did. And so did Isabel and Priti. Lexie refused to apologize, saying they were making a big deal out of nothing.

Anyhow, Isabel's mom, who was the librarian at the school and an amazing person, died last year of cancer, which was awful. Lexie tried to tell Isabel how sorry she was, but Isabel wasn't in the mood to listen to her, and then she ended up leaving the school. Lexie hasn't seen her since.

Some of this I know because I started hanging out with Lexie every day after school once she and Isabel had their thing, and also because I listen when my mom is talking to other moms. You can learn a lot if you pretend to be on your phone or something and just keep quiet.

Priti smiles at Lexie. "Pronounce it any way you like. I just thought you might like to know the *right* way to say it." Priti pulls out her notepad. It has notes written all over it, in different color inks. "Now. We really need to get an idea to present to Pablo."

"Oh, *that's* why you're here," Lexie says, looking directly at me.

Brandon sits up sharply like he sat on a baseball or something, but in his case it just means he's forgotten something. "Movie ideas? Oh, man. I totally spaced on this. I promised Nathan and Mateo I'd help them come up with gags for their project."

He spots them across the lunchroom and jumps up, leaving his half-eaten lunch.

Lexie makes a face. "That's fine, Brandon, we'll just get rid of this mess for you."

I take the tray and dump the contents into a nearby trash can. I don't want to leave the table too long with those two glaring at each other.

Since Priti knows everything, I figure I'll ask her. "Listen, you said you chose me. Did you choose Theo too?"

Priti shakes her head. "That must have been Pablo's idea. I guess he felt Theo would be a good fit for us."

"Umm . . . is it me or is Theo a little . . . ," I begin.

Priti leans in, her eyes wide. "I know, right? What was all that about his phone? And knowing what our parents do?"

Lexie is finishing her lunch, but I know her. She can't stand not being in on this.

And I don't want her to think she's going to lose another friend to Priti.

Not that I'm Isabel Archer, superbrain. But Lexie and I do hang out an awful lot.

I look around the lunchroom to make sure Theo is nowhere to be seen.

I turn to Lexie. "This guy Theo is kinda . . . out there. He acts like he's a superspy or something."

Lexie turns to Priti. "Really? Like how?"

"He has some sort of crazy ultrasecure phone and wears gloves all the time," Priti says.

"He also seems to be able to just, like, appear out of thin air," I say.

Lexie looks up. "Yeah, I see what you mean."

Without having to look, I can feel Theo right behind me.

I *swear* to you I checked the entire lunchroom.

Theo slips into the seat next to Priti. He has no tray.

"Theo, this is Lexie," I say, trying to sound normal.

"Alexandra Mizell. Your father is in advertising. His most recent campaign was working for the nonprofit prisoner's rights group, Call to Action. And your mom is a civil rights attorney."

Lexie nods. "Wow. You know what all our parents do. How about your folks? What do they do?"

Do not mess with Lexie.

"None of your business," Theo says in a matter-of-fact way.

"Seriously," Lexie says. "What do they do?"

"I *am* serious," Theo says.

"Okay, whatever. Who cares what your parents do anyway? I can google it when I get home."

Theo laughs.

Kind of.

A dry *heh*. "Good luck with that."

Priti tries to change the subject. "No tray? You need to eat, right?"

Theo reaches down and pulls up his backpack.

What a shocker. There is a lock on every zipper.

"I never eat the food served at school. There's no telling what they put in there."

He carefully pulls his glove off and places a thumb on one lock and it clicks open.

We watch as Theo takes out a bottle containing a milky brown fluid.

"Soylent," he announces. "It has all the nutrients you need without having to waste time eating."

Oh, I cannot *wait* to hear his ideas for our film.

CHAPTER 12

That Darn Resilience of the Human Spirit

Theo takes a swig of his lunch (yikes) and looks around the emptying lunchroom. "If you ask me, the first thing to do is find out what films the other teams are doing."

I am trying to process the fact that Theo has for the first time said something normal when Priti pulls out her color-coded notes and flourishes them. "Way ahead of you. I have all the other team's ideas right here."

"How did you get this information?" Theo asks, leaning in, clearly impressed. "Hidden microphones? Or a long-range zoom lens to read their lips?"

"I asked them," Priti answers.

Lexie is biting her lip to stop from laughing. I can't believe it, but she and Priti are actually getting along.

Which is a good thing, right? I can't decide yet.

"Let me guess," I say. "Nathan and Mateo are doing a gross-out comedy about a prank war."

Priti checks her notes. "Wow. How did you know?"

"They watch pranking videos, like, twenty-four hours a day," Lexie says before I can answer. "Anybody could have told you that."

"There will no doubt be the obligatory scene of someone being hit in the groin," I feel compelled to add.

Theo takes out his phone and snaps a picture of Priti's notes.

Priti flips over the card. "Apparently they are still discussing what is the most disgusting food to be stuffed into someone's underwear."

"Well, I think you've got your winner right there," Lexie says, and she and Priti laugh.

I'm not sure I like this. It's weird seeing them be so nice to each other.

Priti looks down at her paper. "RPG, Cammi, and Noel are of course writing a fantasy about how characters from their game come to life or something."

I roll my eyes. "Yeah, that's going to work. First of all, where are they going to get the costumes?"

"Don't forget, RPG's dad produces commercials," Lexie says. "He could get them all sorts of props."

Priti picks up the last piece of lettuce from her plate. "Noel *is* always overambitious. Remember his project for last year's science fair?"

Lexie turns to Theo. "He told everyone he was going to build a working electron microscope. He ended up with a series of cardboard tubes and lenses he had borrowed from his dad's lab taped together."

"It was still really cool," I say. "He just didn't have the time or money to do it the way he wanted."

Priti turns to me and grabs my arm. "That's the *thing*! We only have so much time and money to spend. I think their film is never going to get finished."

I barely register what she's saying because, like, *Priti Sharma just grabbed my arm*.

"Who else is there?" Lexie asks.

"Jojo and Oona and Joie—" Priti begins.

"It's about gymnastics," I jump in. "It *has* to be."

"May I finish?" Priti says. "I think this has a chance of winning."

"None of Pablo's students have a chance of winning," I remind her.

"That's what you think," Priti says. "Listen to this: A girl on the team is the best at the vaulting part of the competition. Until she has an accident and gets hurt. All of a sudden, she can't do it anymore. With the help of her coach and her teammates, she faces her fear and digs deep and wins first in the big final meet of the year."

Lexie leans back and nods. "Very inspirational."

"Ex-*act*-ly," Priti says. "She overcomes adversity and it shows the resilience of the human spirit."

Theo looks at his phone. "Movies about sports never win awards. Even inspirational ones."

Priti checks her notes. "*Rocky* . . . *Chariots of Fire* . . . *Million Dollar Baby* . . ."

"Two of those were boxing movies," Theo says. "This is about gymnastics. Totally different."

"Yeah, but you said *sports*," I remind him.

"So what's Beaverton's class doing, if you know everything," Theo snaps at Priti.

"Well—" Priti starts.

"See?" Lexie says, leaning into Theo. "She *does* know everything."

Lexie and Priti giggle. I am generally clueless about girls, but they actually seem to be getting along *really* well.

"Let's see . . . Tony and Fronk"—yes, that's how he spells his name—"are doing some sort of horror film. Beverly, Ramona, and Zuzu are doing something about kids competing in a talent show . . . and um . . ."

Priti pauses. Then she looks at me. "Felix Terrier-Borowitz, Gordon, and Eve are doing something about a girl who starts a movement to stop a big building from being built in the neighborhood before it ruins everything."

"Oh, great," I say. "Let me guess—"

Priti continues. "The villain is a corrupt building commissioner who takes bribes."

I look down and realize my hands have balled into fists. I try to relax them.

"Felix made a point of making sure I wrote that part down," Priti says.

"I bet that one wins the prize," Theo says just because he has to make everything worse.

There is a noise at the door and Priti looks over. Suddenly she sits up straight and brushes a stray hair back into place.

Jensen Wexford from the eighth grade is walking in, golden Thor hair and all.

Jensen is the major crush of all the girls in the seventh grade.

Well, except for Lexie and a few other girls who don't seem all that interested in boys.

He has actually modeled for one of the fashion designers whose kid goes to the school and spotted Jensen at pickup.

You'd think that would make him conceited, but he's a totally chill guy and nice to pretty much everyone.

Jensen cocks his head. "Hey, Priti. I . . . uh . . . thought you were free during lunch."

"Right!" Priti's voice has gone up about two octaves and doesn't sound anything like she normally does. "I am free. Just finishing up with a film class thing here."

"No worries," Jensen says, and unlike most people who say that, it's like he really means it. I don't think Jensen worries about anything.

I know if I looked like him I wouldn't.

Priti gathers together her cards. "Um . . . can we continue this after school? Are you guys okay with that? We can meet at my place."

Theo nods. "I'm okay with that."

"Me too," I say. I'm kind of jazzed to see what kind of place someone like Priti lives in.

"Me three," Lexie says.

"Um, Lexie, this is kind of our meeting," I say.

"No, she should come," Priti says. "I bet she'll have good ideas."

"She's not even in the class," I protest.

Theo takes one last swig of his lunch and turns to look at Priti. "And who's to say she won't give away our idea?"

"Oh, so your idea is going to be this big secret?" Lexie laughs.

"If it's good enough, someone else will want to steal it," Theo says firmly.

Priti looks around the now completely empty lunchroom. "I think we can trust Lexie."

Theo crosses his arms. "I don't trust anybody."

Lexie grabs a card from Priti's pile that doesn't have anything written on it. "Can I borrow your pen?"

She takes Priti's pen and carefully writes out a few sentences. She turns to Priti. "What's today's date?"

Priti tells her, and Lexie continues writing. She turns to Theo. "What's your last name?"

Theo chews his fingernail. "Why do you need to know that?"

"Oh, for crying out loud, Theo!" Priti says, and turns to Lexie. "It's Schatten. S-C-H-A-T-T-E-N."

Lexie nods and goes back to whatever it is she's doing.

"How do you know how to spell my last name?" Theo asks. By this time he's moved on to another finger.

"I always check the kids in my classes in the school parents' guide," Priti says.

"So how come you remember it?" Theo presses her.

I feel the need to educate the new kid. "Theo, Priti remembers *everything.*"

Except that she and I were in two classes together before film.

I guess I am pretty forgettable.

Lexie carefully signs her name.

"There. Now you can trust me."

Theo looks down at the card with suspicion. "What is that?"

Lexie gives him a smug smile. "A nondisclosure agreement."

Theo reads off the card, " 'The undersigned, Lexie Mizell, will hold all conversations and ideas discussed at the meeting on Monday the twentieth of September of Priti Sharma, Alexander Davis, and Theo Schatten in confidence and will not disclose the confidential information discussed to any person or entity without the prior written consent of all three of the parties named above.' "

Theo nods. He looks slightly less concerned.

"Great! See you then!" Priti says, and sweeps out of her chair to join Prince Jensen.

CHAPTER 13

The Priti Palace

As I leave school, I thread my way through throngs of fourth and fifth graders being picked up by their parents or nannies. I try to remember being that age. They seem so small and annoying.

Okay, not as annoying as Violet can be sometimes, but she's still in the lower school, which meets in another building, so I don't have to run into my mom picking her up. Usually I walk home with Lexie. Sometimes I do walk home with Mom and Violet, but I try not to, since Mom is usually chatting with another mom and Violet wants to tell me about her day, which I'll just have to hear about again at dinner when she tells Dad.

My phone vibrates and I take it out to see a text from Priti. It's a group text to me and Theo, giving us her address.

Actually, I'm kind of shocked.

He gave her his number? He seems so paranoid. I assumed he thought texting wasn't secure enough.

I walk up to Lexie, who gives me a "what's up" wave. She had a free period and could have gone home early but there was no way she was going to miss seeing where Priti Sharma lives.

"So where is it?" she asks eagerly. "Down by the water? Columbia Heights?"

Columbia Heights faces the Manhattan skyline across the East River and is filled with old town houses that are some of the most expensive real estate in all of New York.

"You know you could have checked the parents' directory," I say.

Lexie takes a bite from a black-and-white cookie. "Nah, that's cheating."

"By the way, thanks for offering me some," I say, making a grab for it. "Where'd you get it anyway?"

Lexie expertly evades my hand. "I went to Harry's during my free period. Quit it!"

She slaps my hand and carefully breaks off a piece the size of my thumbnail.

I look at the offered crumb. "Wow. Are you sure you can spare that much? I mean, I wouldn't want to deprive you."

Lexie throws her head back and groans. "Okaay. Fine. Here."

She breaks off a slightly larger piece.

This is the snack negotiation we have been going through after school for years.

In her defense, if it was me, I would have eaten the whole thing before she got out of class.

I show her my phone screen. "Willoughby Towers?" she asks.

I point to the two giant glass structures in the distance, looming over downtown Brooklyn. "It's one of those."

Lexie lets out an impressed whistle. "For real? We get to see what they look like from the inside. That is seriously cool."

I give her a smug look. "Oh, *now* you're all into glass towers? I thought you said they were ugly and messed up the neighborhood. But now that Priti lives in one—"

"*You're* the one who said there are good and bad ones," Lexie says, pushing me in the chest. "So shut up."

Since I have no comeback better than "No, *you* shut up," I decide to change the subject.

I hold up my phone screen again. "You missed the most interesting part."

Lexie looks again. "Theo's *number*? Wow. Next thing, he'll be sharing his email."

"I'm pretty sure that's not gonna happen," I answer. "My bet is he will insist on sharing documents online."

"On a secure server!" we both say at the same time, and crack up.

We head down Fulton Street, which brings us out of Brooklyn Heights and into the downtown shopping district.

When I was a little kid, this area was completely different, with mostly small discount stores selling off-brand stuff and sneaker stores and guys on the street yelling for you to get a free cell phone at their store. There were even a few pawnshops.

But then a few high-end clothing labels moved in, and they started this whole run of construction of these luxury high-rise buildings, like Priti's. My dad has been really busy since then. Willoughby Towers are still the tallest, but other ones are popping up just blocks away.

I can hear what my mom would say if she were here: "I can't imagine who has the money to live in these places, but someone has to, because they keep building them."

Brooklyn Heights, like I wrote in my paper, is a landmarked historic district. But the surrounding areas that once were small businesses and warehouses and rooming houses aren't landmarked, so a developer like Mrs. Tolliver's husband and Hugh Hewitt can just come in and tear everything down and put up another big glass tower. And evict people like Mr. Konigsberg. That is, unless the commission my dad sits on says he can't.

Which of course is the whole problem.

We cross Boerum Place, which is the six-lane thoroughfare that divides the downtown shopping district from the Heights, and head over to Priti's glass palace.

We walk up to the lobby, where a doorman greets us. I swear it's as big as my whole house in here. The ceiling is like four stories high. Late afternoon sunlight pours in from the windows, and the tiled floor echoes with our footsteps as we walk what feels like three blocks just to get to the reception desk.

There is a woman behind the desk. She is young and in a black blazer with a black T-shirt. She has MAYUMI embossed on the nametag on her lapel.

"Can I help you?" Mayumi asks.

I decide to let Lexie handle the formalities.

I mean, she would anyway, but it doesn't bother me.

"Sharma, please." Lexie motions for me to show her my phone. She checks it. "Apartment 2012."

Mayumi presses a few buttons on the console in front of her. She calls up to the apartment. "Yes, I have . . ." She looks at us. "Are you two together?"

"No!" Lexie says quickly.

I shake my head. "She doesn't mean like that. Yes, we are both here to see Priti Sharma."

"Right. Of course. Lexie and Alex," Lexie says.

"And Theo," says *you know who*, who has materialized from out of nowhere as usual.

As Mayumi confers with someone in the apartment, I turn to Theo. "How did you do that? Why didn't we hear your footsteps on the tile floor?"

"I'm very good," Theo says simply.

Not like a brag, just like a fact.

No kidding.

Mayumi has been typing something on her keyboard. She reaches up and has a small ball-like object in her hand.

"You're all set," she announces. "I just need to snap your pictures and we can get you upstairs."

Theo's thumbnail is in his mouth. "You don't need a picture of all of us, right? Just one of us. Right?"

Mayumi smiles. "Sorry, I need all of you. No one gets into the building without us doing this."

"Maybe we can meet across the street at the burger place," Theo suggests quickly.

"Jeez, Theo, relax," Lexie says. "There is no way I'm not going up there. What's the big deal?"

Theo leans in to talk to the woman. "Listen. You delete these photos after we leave. Is that correct?"

"We don't usually, but we *can*," Mayumi says. "But that means we'd have to take another picture when you come back."

"That's fine," Theo says. "I'm never coming back."

Mayumi gives Theo a smile. "That's a shame."

"Just take the picture," Theo growls.

"Don't mind him," Lexie says quickly. "He's just kind of a nut about privacy."

Theo shoots Lexie a look as Mayumi clicks photos of the three of us.

"I totally get it," Mayumi answers. "These days you can't be too careful."

Theo grunts an assent.

"Thank you very much," I say, trying for damage control.

Mayumi hands us little cards with our photos printed on them. "No problem. Elevator bank H-3. Just get in when it arrives. It will take you to your floor."

There is a kind of turnstile thing we have to go through to get to the elevators. We insert our cards in the slot and it spits it out on the other side as the partition opens to let us pass.

Theo nods approvingly.

Lexie can't resist. "See? It's all about security. Isn't that something you can appreciate?"

"I could bypass this system so easily if I wanted," he says.

I can't tell if he's full of it or if he's serious.

Either way, he's definitely the most unique kid I've ever met.

And I go to a school with a boy who last year wore a fake handlebar mustache for an entire semester. And no one said anything because, "Hey, it's Saint Anselm's."

So when I say that . . .

CHAPTER 14

We Reach a Consensus: My Idea Is Brilliant, Yours Is Stupid

The elevator is like a solid steel cube, with a small window that shows our desired floor. As we whoosh up, Lexie can't resist. "So now we have your phone number, aren't you afraid of what we'll learn about you?"

Theo doesn't even turn around, but his pale face and self-satisfied smile are reflected back at us on all the surfaces. "Only a fool would give out his real number. Do I look like a fool?"

I was going to say "You look like a Marvel supervillain in training," but I figured he wouldn't get the reference. "Nah, I wouldn't go that far."

Theo reaches into his pocket and fishes out a cheap-looking phone.

"You ever heard of a burner phone?" he asks.

"Like the kidnappers use in cheesy movies?" Lexie says.

"Like anyone who wants to keep his information private uses," snorts Theo. "I got this one just for our project."

The doors slide open and we arrive at the front door of the Sharma residence. Or one of them. I'm willing to bet Priti's family has more than one residence. Like probably six.

There is a camera aimed at us as I ring the buzzer. Theo looks uncomfortable and hides his face behind a curtain of hair.

The door swings open and Priti is standing there. "Welcome, you guys! Come in, come in!"

She has changed her clothes from what she was wearing at school. She is now wearing a T-shirt and jeans.

"Nice T-shirt," Lexie says.

I then realize it's exactly the same T-shirt Lexie wears. The one with the *Powerpuff Girls* on it. I can be excused for not realizing it at first because it looks so different on Priti. It's not just that she accessorized it with a necklace and bracelets. It's a lot tighter and looks like a fashion statement. I think about mentioning this out loud and then I remember that I want to live.

Priti looks down and laughs. "Oh, yeah. When I saw yours the other day, I really liked it so I went online and ordered one for myself. I hope you don't mind."

Lexie looks down. "No, it's totally fine. You look really good in it," she murmurs, sounding all shy for some reason.

Priti takes Lexie's hand and pulls her into the apartment, with me and Theo following behind. "Come on, you guys, we just *have* to get this idea done!"

Priti stops as we turn from the entryway and face the living room. "Okay," she sighs, "I guess you have to see the view first. Ta-da!"

Definitely worth a *ta-da*. The windows go from floor to ceiling and present a view of all of downtown Brooklyn, with the East River and then Manhattan beyond that. The afternoon sun is even more impressive up here than it was in the lobby, glinting off the cars and glass storefronts below us, sparkling like water.

Up here, with the thick windows, there is no traffic noise, no people yelling into their cell phones, no sirens.

Just quiet. I turn and see the luxurious leather furniture and what looks like priceless artwork on the walls. There is a large square coffee table in the middle of the room, with pads of paper and pens laid out.

Lined up next to them are glass bowls filled with nuts of all kinds, chips, and a tray with different kinds of vegetables cut up next to some sort of dip.

"I didn't know what snacks you liked," Priti says anxiously. "I hope these are okay."

"It's great," I assure her. "Everything's great!"

Lexie nods but doesn't say anything else. Which is so not her. It's like she's a different person in here.

Theo has been looking around the room with a practiced

eye. He points to a print on the wall. "That's a real Matisse, isn't it?"

"Good eye, young man!"

A woman who I assume is Priti's mom has swept into the room. I know it's corny to say "Mother? I thought you were her older sister!" to someone's mom, but in this case it's true. Except for the fact that her hair is pulled back and she's wearing expensive workout clothes, they have like the exact same face and practically the same voice. "Alex . . . Theo . . . Lexie . . . this is my mom," Priti says.

Priti's mom grabs a water bottle from the bar area and swings a gym bag over her shoulder. "Darling, have a productive meeting. Lovely to meet all of you!" She turns to Priti and says, "I'll be back at five-thirty," and kisses her lightly on the forehead.

Priti watches her go, and we hear the front door snap shut.

"There's a gym in the building?" Lexie asks.

At first Priti looks at her like *duh,* and then her expression changes. "Um, yeah. It's nice so you don't have to get all sweaty and then walk home . . . you know . . ."

Theo has already seated himself in one of the poufy leather chairs gathered around the coffee table and helped himself to a handful of nuts.

"Hey, Theo, could you use one of those small plates? And a napkin? Also, anyone want something to drink? Seltzer?" Priti asks.

"Sounds great," I say. "Then we really need to get to work."

"So, here's *my* idea," Priti begins after bringing us our selt-zers. "I mean, we don't have to go with it, but I figured some-one should go first."

"I'm sure it's amazing!" Lexie says, which is definitely not what she would have said to me.

We lean in, pens at the ready.

"So a girl has a crush on this older boy, and she pretends to be all sorts of things she isn't because she thinks he likes that kind of girl. Right? Like she pretends to be dumber than she really is, or all mysterious. But ultimately, none of those things work, and she finds out that once she starts just being herself, smart and funny and quirky, he falls for her." Priti looks at us. "Perfect, right?"

None of us knows what to say.

Finally, I feel the need to let Priti down easy. "It makes me want to throw up."

Lexie adds little gagging noises. Ah, the Lexie I know has returned.

Priti is not used to being made fun of. "So . . . you don't *like* it?"

Theo has been looking out the window. "I can see my house from here."

"What's wrong with it?" Priti demands.

"You . . . read a *lot* of YA rom-coms, don't you?" Lexie says. "I mean, it's like the plot of a hundred of those."

Priti pouts. "How do *you* know?"

Lexie gives her a side-eye. "Priti, you're not the only one who reads. I read *everything*."

"We are not doing a dumb love story," Theo announces. "Because they never win awards."

Priti sighs. "Okay, that's fair. I mean, it happens to be an *awesome* idea, but I take your point."

"I think it should be really funny," I suggest. "Too bad those other guys thought of the prank idea."

"Funny is good," Lexie says, "but not dumb guy humor. Something satirical. You know, like a takeoff on a famous movie."

"Yeah!" For the first time Theo sounds interested. "Maybe we could do a horror film."

"Theo, Tony and Fronk in the other class are already doing one," Priti says.

"But what if ours is better?" Theo presses her.

"They're just going to say we're copying them," I say. "Besides, how scary could we make it and not have Beaverton throw a fit?"

Theo crosses his idea off on his pad. "Yeah, I guess you're right. But it's too bad. I know where we could get really realistic body parts."

None of us are going to ask him about this, so we move on.

"So if the girls are doing inspirational, and RPG and his friends are doing some kind of fantasy thing, what's left?" I ask.

"Look, we have to come up with something," Priti says. "I have to get to my homework."

"Have you done that paper on 'Beowulf' yet?" Lexie asks her.

Priti falls back on the couch. "Gah! That is so hard! And it's due the same week we have a presentation in science!"

"I've got a French test on Friday followed by a math quiz," I add. "With one on the tenth floor and the other on the third! With like five minutes to get there!"

"Do you guys ever get used to running up and down all the stairs?" Theo asks. "I don't think any other school has that."

"Not really. Especially with all those little kids getting in the way all the time," Lexie says.

I pick up a chip and wave it at the others. "And the high schoolers making out in hallways! I mean, get a room!"

"And how about the lunches. Why do they always try so hard to be *different*?" Priti asks.

Lexie holds her hand up. "Guys! Guys! That's it!"

We look at each other.

"What's it?" I ask.

"Your idea. This is it," Lexie says.

Priti starts to scribble something on her pad, as fast as she can. "All the things that drive us crazy about Saint Anselm's— I love it!"

Theo has started to chew his thumbnail again. "I dunno . . . It sounds promising . . . but tricky."

"Yeah," I say. "I just don't see the teachers and administrators letting us do it."

"It can't just be a list of stuff. It has to have some sort of structure . . . ," Priti muses.

"How do real filmmakers get away with it?" Lexie asks.

"By being funny," Theo suggests.

"So what kind of story . . . what has classic structure?" I ask.

"The Bible?" Theo suggests.

Priti laughs. "Oh, yeah. That's going to be really non-controversial."

"How about . . . a fairy tale?" Lexie says.

"The three little pigs?" Priti throws out.

"The three little filmmakers and the Big Bad Teacher?" I say, and we all crack up.

"That would be *epic*," Lexie says. "Oh my gosh. Can you imagine Beaverton's face?"

Theo looks worried. "Do we really want to risk ticking him off that badly?"

Priti crosses her arms. "Okay, Theo, you have a problem with everyone else's ideas. What's yours?"

Theo thinks for a second. "Cinderella. When she fits in the glass slipper, she gets to go to the college of her choice."

"And you thought my love story idea was dumb," Priti grumbles.

"What's wrong with it? We have the evil stepsisters cutting off their toes like in the real fairy tale to try and fit into the shoe!" Theo says, jumping up.

"Yeah, but what about—" Lexie tries.

"Wait! It's perfect! See, it's a metaphor, like when kids try to be someone else just to get into college."

"Or try to be someone else to win their crush," I say. "It's the same story. It's not about Saint Anselm's. I think you just want to do something with blood and body parts."

Theo sits down. "Maybe . . ."

Priti glances at her pad. "We've got *nothing*. And I have homework."

"We all do," Lexie says, and we gather our stuff.

Priti checks her watch. "I'm late! I'm late! For a very important date!"

Lexie stops in the front area and turns around. "What did you say?"

Priti shrugs. "Just something my mom and I always say when we're running late. It's from . . ."

Priti stops and stares at Lexie and a smile breaks out on her face. "You think?"

Lexie nods. "It's perfect."

Priti takes out her pad. "You know, it is."

"What is?" Theo demands.

Lexie is looking over Priti's shoulder as she writes something. Priti shows it to Lexie and they both giggle. "That is *so* great!"

"I know, right?" Lexie says, sounding once again very un-Lexie-like. I swear she looks like she's glowing. But it could just be the late afternoon sun.

"You guys want to include us, or just continue being obnoxious?" I ask.

Priti turns over her pad and I read what's on it.

You know what?

It *is* perfect.

CHAPTER 15

Down the Rabbit Hole

Written on the pad is *Alice in Anselmland.*

I can tell that even Theo is impressed. "Yeah. That could be really fun."

The front door opens.

In our old run-down house, when someone comes in, it takes forever between the two different locks and the wobbly doorknob on the inside door. Here, it's kind of a crisp *ka-thunk* that sounds expensive, like a luxury car door or something. As Priti's mom comes and kisses Priti before running off to the shower (of course, first telling us how happy she is to have met us), I gaze one last time at the beautiful brand-new kitchen, the dazzling view, and the enormous windows and take in the general quiet.

It makes you understand why people want to live in these kinds of buildings. My mom always looks at them from the outside and calls them "cold and soulless" and tells my dad how much she'd rather have "charm and history," but when the radiator goes out, or the toilet clogs for the fifth time that week (Violet has a newfound love of toilet paper), even she has to admit that Old House Charm has its limits.

Priti calls for the elevator, and then we say our goodbyes.

In the hushed hallway, Theo turns to Lexie and me. "It's a really good idea."

"Yeah, I *know*," Lexie says. "Now aren't you glad I came with you guys?"

I snort. "It wasn't your idea."

"It totally was," Lexie says, getting red in the face, like she does when I accuse her of cheating at *Mario Kart*.

"It doesn't matter whose idea it was," Theo breaks in. "The important thing is that we discuss it with *no one*."

"Like someone is going to steal the idea?" Lexie asks as the doors open, and we step into the elevator.

There is already a kid in there with a squash racket. Clearly heading to their private lesson at the Heights Squash Club, a fancy members-only place where people like us only go as guests, if at all.

"Theo, everyone has already come up with their ideas," protests Lexie. "So no one is going to—"

A look from Theo cuts her off. He motions with his eyes to our fellow occupant. The kid has AirPods firmly in his ears and is clearly not listening.

The doors open and we all pile out. We start out the door and Theo stops us, waiting until the kid goes out the door and turns right.

As we go through the turnstiles, I trade stares with Lexie. "Okay, Theo, what was that all about?"

"You never know who's listening," he says simply.

Lexie unwraps a piece of gum and puts it in her mouth. "Theo. Seriously. Chill. Out. He doesn't even go to our school."

Theo looks at Lexie like she's Violet's age. "Yeah, so? You don't know that he doesn't have friends who go to Saint Anselm's. And one of them could be in our class."

"He was listening to music!" I protest.

"You don't know that," Theo says. "Did you hear any music leaking out of his AirPods? I didn't. That's the oldest trick in the book. Pretend to be listening to music so people let down their guard and talk in front of you."

"Okay, so everybody in the world wants this brilliant idea of ours," I answer. "What do you suggest?"

"I'm just saying you can't be too careful."

"Your parents are CIA, aren't they?" Lexie asks.

Theo doesn't smile. "You'll never know."

Lexie turns and offers me a piece of gum.

I take the gum and we go to leave the building.

Theo is already gone.

"How does he do that?" Lexie marvels.

Listening to our sneakers squeak as they pull against the marble floor, I wonder myself.

"Maybe he was trained by ninjas," I suggest.

Usually Lexie would laugh, but today she just looks up and down Livingston Street.

Theo is nowhere to be seen.

She turns to me. "He is kind of freaking me out."

"As long as he helps us make a good movie, I'm cool with it," I say. "But it is definitely going to take some getting used to."

/////

"So who's writing the script?" my dad asks.

We're walking on the Promenade after dinner. It's a beautiful long walkway overlooking the same majestic view of the Manhattan skyline that those expensive town houses have, but it's free and filled with benches. Mom and Violet have gone on ahead to a nearby playground.

I shrug. "We all are."

"Hmm . . ." My dad sounds like he wants to say something but at the same time *doesn't* want to say it.

"Is that a problem?" I ask.

"Has Pablo talked to you guys about collaboration?"

I think for a second. "Well . . . sure. I mean, about how everyone working on a film has to be making the same film."

My dad nods. I'm not sure he gets it.

"Obviously they're making the same film. Right? 'Cause they're working on the project together. But I think he was talking about agreeing on the tone of it, and the point of view."

My dad hides a smile. "Yes, I figured that's what he meant."

"It's okay, I wasn't sure what he meant at first too," I say, not totally convinced he's telling the truth. But he *is* a pretty smart guy.

We pass the benches filled with old couples sipping coffee and tourists taking selfies or setting up expensive camera tripods to take that perfect picture of the Manhattan skyline at sunset with the Brooklyn Bridge in the background that's only been taken a million times before (but I guess not by them?). The calm pleasant atmosphere is spoiled by a figure thrusting a paper into the hands of all the innocent people on the benches.

It's Mr. Konigsberg. He's wearing the same dirty corduroy jacket. I have a feeling it's the only one he owns.

He's yelling the same thing over and over: "Meeting to stop Court Street Towers! Preserve Brooklyn Heights and stop overdevelopment!"

Most people are polite and take the flyer, and only fold it over or crumple it up after he moves on.

He sees my dad and me and walks past us without saying anything.

"Hey," I say, trying to change the mood. "That's Felix in like fifty years."

My dad doesn't laugh. "Don't make fun of Felix. He's an idealist."

I grit my teeth. "But he's so annoying. Like if you don't agree with him about everything, you're an awful, uncaring person."

"I know. Sometimes people are so passionate about

their cause they see everyone else as an enemy. That's the hard part."

"So you agree with him about the project?" I ask.

My dad shakes his head. "I honestly need more information. People like Felix sometimes need to be careful where they're getting their facts. It's too easy to hear something and just take it as true if it fits the way you see the world."

I realize my dad is looking at Mr. Konigsberg, who is arguing loudly with a woman in leggings walking a designer dog.

"You know, I met that guy," I tell Dad. "Lexie introduced me. He got kicked out of his building so Hugh Hewitt could tear it down and put up one of his—"

"Alex, please. I get enough of this at work," my dad says, cutting off any further conversation on this topic.

Dad turns to gaze out over the water. "Let's get back to your film. Reaching a consensus isn't always easy. You're going to have to compromise, you know."

"Dad, it's not like I don't have a little sister," I remind him. "I wanted to go to the skate park, and she wanted to go to the playground. So we're going to the playground."

"Not that kind of compromise," he says. "This is more about genuinely believing that your way is better but having to take others' ideas into consideration. If you're too rigid, people aren't going to want to work with you."

I'm starting to realize this conversation is more about my dad and his work than my silly film script.

I put my head on his arm. "Sure, Dad. I hear you."

He comes out of his thoughts and looks down at me and

smiles. "Wow. You're almost up to my shoulder. You really grew this summer."

I hadn't really stood next to my dad like this in a while. "Yeah, I guess you're right. Most of the guys in my class are so much taller than me I guess I didn't notice."

We hear a familiar scream. It's bloodcurdling, but nothing we haven't heard a thousand times.

"It sounds like your sister has found the swings," my dad observes.

CHAPTER 16

Nice Try, Mr. Beaverton

As soon as I get to film class, I see that Priti and Theo have already gotten started.

Priti has her laptop open and is pecking away furiously. "That's good!"

Without looking up, she addresses me. "Theo gave me something great: You know the scene where Alice sees the cake with the card that says 'eat me' and she does and that makes her shrink? What if instead of cake, it's meat loaf from the lunchroom and she eats it and *thinks* it's going to make her small, and instead she just gets sick?"

Theo has a slightly stunned look on his face, like no one's ever liked an idea of his in his entire life.

"Sure!" I say enthusiastically. "But I thought we were supposed to be working on this together."

Priti looks guilty for a nanosecond. Then she brightens. "We *were* working together. Now we're working together with *you*."

I decide not to make a big deal out of this. "Look, let's just agree that all three of us should be deciding stuff that goes in, okay?"

"No problem," Theo says, "but you liked the idea so why are you making a big deal out of this?"

"I am *not* making a big deal out of this," I say a little too loudly.

Jojo yells over from the corner. "Hey, you guys, we're trying to write over here."

"Like you didn't just kick me in the head doing a backflip," grouses RPG.

"To be honest, the noise level in the room is pretty high," Pablo says as he ducks to avoid Joie doing a forward roll. "And doing gymnastics in the classroom is a little dangerous."

"But it helps us think," Oona whines.

"And we're not hurting anyone," Joie adds.

"That's what you think," RPG says, rubbing his head.

Jojo rolls her eyes. "Don't be such a baby, Ralph."

I turn back to my partners and find both of them glued to their phones.

"Hey! Can we focus on our movie, please?" I say, annoyed.

Both hold their phones out to me wordlessly. On each screen is an e-book of *Alice's Adventures in Wonderland*.

Oops.

"So there's this scene where she meets a caterpillar who's smoking from a water pipe."

"That could be where Alice goes down the back stairs by mistake and bumps into a kid vaping!" I suggest.

Priti turns to her laptop. "Perfect."

Theo looks skeptical. "Are they gonna let us put that in?"

"Look, vaping is a big problem in the school," I explain. "As long as we show that it's a gross and disgusting habit, I think we're good."

Priti nods. "How about the Mad Hatter's tea party?"

"I have Bergstrom for history!" Theo exclaims. He doesn't have to say anything else. Roger Bergstrom is famous at school for wearing the most bizarre hats, like a huge furry Russian hat with earflaps in the winter. And he's really funny. I had him last year.

"Alice could open a door into the faculty lounge," Priti adds. "And we could have a bunch of teachers inside."

"And the Cheshire cat *has* to be Mrs. Whitman," I say.

Priti nods, and even Theo manages to smile.

Mrs. Whitman is the secretary in the middle school office, who's always grinning and disappearing right when you need to ask her something important.

Pablo comes up to our desk and we go over our ideas with him. He laughs a few times, and then looks serious.

"You three have come up with something great here. I have a few suggestions for films you should watch to get inspired. But be careful that this isn't just a bunch of jokes."

"Is there something wrong with that?" I ask. "As long as they're funny?"

Pablo stops for a second and is clearly trying to find the right way to answer me. I like that about him. "Alex, being funny is all well and good, but using humor to make a larger point is really powerful."

I can't resist. "You mean like those guys?" I say, pointing to Nathan and Mateo, who are busy figuring out whether they can find a way to make it look like someone stapled their lips together.

Pablo shakes his head. "Alex, sometimes funny is just funny for funny's sake. *But.* If you can point out the things that are wrong with the school and make us laugh at the same time, now *that* would be truly amazing."

He walks toward his desk. And then he turns back. "I think you have the opportunity to make something really important here. And I think you are the ones who can do it."

Inspired, we get back to work.

We are making a list of all the things that bug us about Saint Anselm's, when suddenly I look up.

"I feel a great disturbance in the Force, as if millions of voices suddenly cried out in terror and were suddenly silenced," I intone.

"Huh?" Theo says.

"It's a *Star Wars* reference," I explain.

"Oh, I know the line. I just didn't know why you were saying Obi-Wan Kenobi's line as Princess Leia," he says.

Can I help it if my voice hasn't changed yet?

"I do a *great* Obi-Wan impression," I grumble.

"I thought it was perfect," says Priti, who was probably just being polite. "But why did you say it?"

I gesture to the front of the room, where the dark presence of Mr. Beaverton is looking over Pablo.

They are deep in discussion.

Theo chews his fingernail. "Why is he here? He has his own class to teach."

"And why do they keep looking over at us?" Priti asks.

Pablo does not look happy. He keeps waving his hands dismissively, but Mr. Beaverton simply stands there, impassive.

We finally hear his rumbling ominous voice. "Pablo, you have to tell them."

They walk over to our desks.

I had never been so close to Mr. Beaverton before. He has a weird smell. Like a mixture of pipe tobacco and some aftershave they sold in the seventies. It's like the odor's been trapped in his clothes all these years and couldn't escape.

"Listen, kids, something's come up—" Pablo begins.

Mr. Beaverton cuts him off. "Miss Sharma. I believe you know Jensen Wexford."

Priti looks right at him, concerned. "Yes, of course. Is he all right?"

Pablo jumps in. "He's fine. This isn't about him. It's about his brother."

Priti looks confused. "Sean?"

Mr. Beaverton looks gleeful. "Aha! So you admit you know him!"

"Of course she knows him," I say. "He's like the most popular boy in the senior class. We all know him."

Mr. Beaverton hasn't taken his eyes off Priti. It's creepy. "I wasn't talking to you. I was talking to Miss Sharma."

"So what if I do?" Priti sounds annoyed. I'm not sure I would be so defiant to a teacher, especially one like Mr. Beaverton. But this *is* Priti Sharma we're talking about.

"Here's the thing," Pablo says. "Mr. Beaverton was reminding me that when Sean took this course, he did a film with a similar premise to yours."

"And?" Priti demands.

"It's just that—" Pablo sighs.

Beaverton once more cuts in. "You cannot take another student's idea for a film. That's plagiarism, just as if you took another student's paper."

Now it's my turn to be annoyed. "What? We didn't take anyone's idea. We came up with this ourselves."

"I'm sorry, I find that hard to believe," Mr. Beaverton says, with no indication that he's sorry at all. Actually he sounds like he's enjoying this. "But it's not your fault. Pablo should have alerted you to this earlier. I'm sorry you have to find another idea after all the work you've put into this one."

Pablo is looking at the floor. He won't meet our eyes.

Mr. Beaverton *actually* rubs his hands together like some corny villain. "Well, now that that's settled—"

"Actually, we're doing *Alice in Anselmland* and you're not going to stop us," Theo says.

I kind of forgot Theo was here, to be honest.

Beaverton looks at Theo as if *he's* seeing him for the first time.

"I beg your pardon, Mr. Schatten. Perhaps at your other schools—the ones that kicked you out—you spoke to teachers that way. At Saint Anselm's we don't."

Ouch. If that comment bothered Theo, he doesn't show it. "Yeah, whatever. I've never been accused of plagiarizing my own idea."

"No one is accusing *you* of anything." Mr. Beaverton leans in to confront Theo. "Priti Sharma stole that idea."

Before Priti can say anything, Theo turns his laptop around. On it is a video screen. It says *Student Project: Sean Wexford, Konrad Houser, Jemma Kincaid—"Mother Anselm's Nursery Rhymes."*

Mr. Beaverton's eyes widen. "How did you get that? It's in a private archive."

"Yeah." Theo sniffs. "The password was easy to guess. You have all the Golden Reel's winning films going back to the beginning. I watched them all. Some of them were pretty good."

"You hacked into our database?" Pablo asks, sounding both angry and more than a little impressed.

"I wouldn't call it *hacking*," Theo says. "I mean, all I did was put in the right password and—"

"You are going right to the head of school," Mr. Beaverton thunders, so loud the entire room falls silent.

"Fifty points to Slytherin," Noel says from the corner.

Which I normally would find pretty funny, but considering the situation, I wasn't in the mood to laugh.

Theo seems amazingly calm.

Maybe because he's been kicked out of so many other schools?

"I don't think so," he says simply. "You just accused us of plagiarism. Let's look at this film, shall we?"

"That won't be necessary," Mr. Beaverton snaps.

Theo looks Mr. Beaverton directly in the eye. "I didn't think so. Because we both know this is a fairy tale, not *Alice in Wonderland*. And what's more, this one is just about how hard it is to be our age going through all the stuff we have to go through while *our* movie is all about Saint Anselm's."

Theo pulls down his laptop lid with a snap. "I mean, they sound a bit alike, but they're totally different premises. Don't you agree?"

Pablo turns to Mr. Beaverton, who is clearly trying to decide how to answer this. "Let's just say . . . you might have misremembered Sean's film."

Mr. Beaverton answers his younger colleague without turning. "What?"

"An honest mistake," Pablo suggests.

Mr. Beaverton holds his gaze on Theo. "I don't often make mistakes, young man. If I were you, I'd remember that."

And with that, he turns on his heel and stomps off.

I read that phrase in a book someplace, but I've never actually seen someone turn on their heel in real life.

It's kind of graceful and silly at the same time. A little dramatic.

We all look at Theo, impressed.

Priti, maybe for the first time in her life, is speechless.

The bell rings.

Finally Pablo speaks. "Theo, glad you cleared up our misunderstanding. Just promise me you won't pull a stunt like that again."

"I was just doing research," Theo says, laying a gloved hand on his laptop.

CHAPTER 17

You Have a Beautiful Glabella

I swear, Lexie's eyes are, like, *glowing* as Priti relates what happened in film class.

Somehow, it's still weird that Priti sits with us at lunch now instead of with her cool girl posse. If it were anyone else, they'd probably give her a hard time about deserting them, but since it's Priti, they're cool with it. Because she rules.

Lexie turns to Theo, who is calmly sipping on his gross (as if I need to remind anyone) lunch. "Whoa, I didn't peg you as a savage! Man, Beaverton must be so ticked off!"

"He said something about you being kicked out of other schools," I begin.

Theo shoots me a freezing look. "Say it louder. I don't think the kids at the table in the corner heard you."

"Lots of kids come here from other schools," Priti says, daintily eating her sloppy joe. Yeah, I have no idea how someone can daintily eat that either. It even has the word *sloppy* in the name. "Nobody's going to hold it against you."

Theo answers her in a flat voice, but there's real anger behind it. "Nobody needs to know my business. Beaverton had no right to say that."

"Hey, you made a point of showing him up," I say. "Beaverton isn't the type to play nice."

Theo's pale face registers the slightest amount of color somewhere in the vicinity of his cheeks. "He was accusing Priti of *plagiarism*. I wasn't going to let that happen."

Lexie takes a not-so-dainty chomp out of her sloppy joe. She notices the look of distaste on Priti's face and grabs my napkin to blot the juice running down her chin. "Whatever, Theo. I think most kids would say Beaverton's had it coming forever."

"Let's just forget it," Theo says. "Can we talk about the movie? We need to split up the scenes."

We've decided that the best way to write the script is to each write a first draft of different scenes and then come back and discuss how to make them better.

Priti flips open her binder and takes out blue, red, and green pens.

"One color for each of us," she announces. Just then, her nose wrinkles. "Um, wow. Someone's wearing—"

Lexie points with her fork. "Brandon Mullford at twelve o'clock."

Brandon arrives about a minute after his body spray and

sits down with an extremely sloppy tray heaped with sloppy joes. "Hey it's Theo! The legend!"

Theo eyes Brandon but doesn't say anything.

"I wish I had been there!" Brandon exclaims. "Just to see the Beaverman's face."

Lexie leans over and grabs a napkin from the pile Brandon has brought with him (this isn't his first sloppy joe rodeo) and wipes off the remaining yuck from the front of her shirt.

I should mention that I finished my lunch before we started the meeting because I am very good at time management. Also I had a free period before and got here early so I could be sure I didn't spill anything on myself during lunch with Priti.

And Theo, of course.

Not just Priti.

I mean, I felt my ideas would be taken more seriously if I didn't have a huge red blotch on my T-shirt. Lexie clearly didn't have such qualms.

"Brandon, these guys are going to work on their movie," Lexie says. "Maybe you should leave."

Brandon snorts. "So how come you get to stay?"

"Because I'm not helping Nathan and Mateo with their movie, that's why."

Brandon takes his tray and gets up. "Cool. Well, you guys don't have to work so hard, because no way you're going to win the award. *Crotch Tape* is going to be awesome."

"*Crotch Tape?*" I say, putting those two words together in a sentence for the first time in my life.

"That's the name of Mateo and Nathan's movie. It's such an awesome title." Brandon registers our blank faces. "You know, like Scotch tape, only it's—"

"We get it," Lexie says. "We just don't want it."

"You're just jealous you didn't think of it," Brandon says, and moves off to join the two creative geniuses who came up with *Crotch Tape*.

Theo watches him go. "Amazing. His father won the Pulitzer Prize for journalism in 2014."

"You really know what everyone's father or mother does?" Priti asks.

"Information is power," Theo says, screwing on the cap of his lunch.

"I guess that makes you a regular Thanos," Lexie says, and I have to crack up.

Theo stares at her.

"He's . . . um . . . the bad guy from the *Avengers* movies," Lexie explains.

Theo nods. "I've heard of them."

Priti clears her throat. "Guys. Let's get this done. Lunch is almost over."

We each have our favorite scenes. I get the Mad Hatter's tea party, which I am super psyched about. Theo is taking the beginning, because he doesn't know that much about the school yet. Priti is taking the student lounge scene, and we keep going through the rest of the outline.

"Remember what Pablo said," I remind them. "It can't

just be funny. If we're doing it right, each joke has to make a point."

Priti wordlessly holds up her notebook. On an earlier page from this morning, she's written in big letters *EACH JOKE MUST MAKE A POINT.*

"Okay, fine," I say. I guess Priti doesn't need to be reminded of anything.

Lexie looks at our outline. "So . . . there are a lot of roles in this. I mean *a lot.* How are you going to get kids to be in it?"

Priti smiles. "I don't think that will be a problem. I can be pretty persuasive. Also, for the older kids, Jensen says he'll get his brother to talk them into it."

Theo looks worried. "Yeah, but getting kids in it—and teachers too—is only part of it, right? We have to make sure they can all be there at the same time."

"That's true," I say. "Half the boys have soccer practice after school, and a lot of the girls too. Or basketball."

Priti doesn't seem overly concerned. "It just means being organized."

Lexie laughs. "Oh, that's all it takes!" Then she looks at Priti's face and realizes she wasn't joking. "I mean, sure. You've got your binders and everything."

"And different colored pens," I add, because I feel like I should say something.

"I'll draw up a tentative cast list," Priti says, "and email it to you guys."

"No email, remember?" Theo says. "Just put it up on

Postbox. I have a secure account with TFA, which you'll need to set up through my laptop."

"TFA?" I ask.

Theo answers like I just asked "Why is the sky blue, Daddy?"

"Two-factor authorization. Usually I would insist on multi-factor authorization, but since this is lower security, two should be sufficient."

He's pulled out his laptop, which is of course covered in a black armor skin that looks like you could drop it from Priti's apartment and it would bounce off the pavement.

He boots it up and stares at the screen. "Biometrics," he announces. "Fingerprint and iris scanning."

He then turns to us. "Um, Lexie, could you excuse us?"

I thought Lexie was going to say something smart, but instead she picks up her tray. "Sure, Theo. I'll just bus my tray. Can I take yours as well?"

I am about to faint from shock and hand mine over when I realize that she's talking to Priti.

Priti hands her tray over and gives Lexie a dazzling smile. "That's super nice, Lexie. Thanks!"

Lexie returns her smile weakly and heads off, looking dazzled.

Yeah, I don't think Priti is going to have much trouble getting other kids to be in our movie. Or teachers. Or parents. She's so charming and gorgeous she could probably get movie stars to be in it.

I'm pulled back to reality when Theo snaps his fingers in front of my face. "Hey! Alex! Priti is all set up. I need your voice."

"My voice?" I screech. I am kind of sensitive about my voice these days.

"For voice authentication," Theo explains. "Your laptop has a microphone, right?"

"Of course," I say.

"Just lean right in and say your name. It's very sensitive."

Like I'm not? I do what I'm told and say my name. I cringe when Theo plays it back. I sound like a little girl.

"Now we need to set a password," Theo declares.

"How about *Jabberwocky*?" I suggest.

Theo snorts. "Too easy."

"Really?" I say. "Who is guessing here, anyway?"

Priti is writing different things down. "It is kind of the first thing I'd try."

"AnselmLandRosenstein?" I offer.

Theo shakes his head. "Come on, that's like *so* obvious."

Priti looks up from her binder and announces: "Lutwidge11261865."

Theo nods. "That's more like it." He looks over her shoulder to copy it down.

"You want to explain what it means?" I ask.

Priti looks at me with disappointment. "Alex. Think."

I hate it when people say that.

"Umm . . . it has to do with *Alice in Wonderland,* I guess."

Theo looks up from his screen. "Lewis Carroll's real name was Charles Lutwidge Dodgson, and the first edition of *Alice's Adventures in Wonderland* came out November twenty-sixth, 1865."

"You just looked that up," I say.

"Yeah . . . but"—Theo looks over at Priti—"you just *knew* that, didn't you?"

We both stare at her.

"I like to know things," she says.

I remember in class whenever she and Isabel Archer would throw in something incredible that no one else in class knew (like the fact that that space between your eyebrows is called the *glabella*. Who knows these things in fourth grade? Isabel and Priti did), they'd say the same thing.

Lexie approaches the table. "Is it safe to come back?"

Theo nods. "Sure, everything is set up."

"I bet I can guess the password," Lexie says as she watches Theo close the tabs on his browser.

Priti scoots over so Lexie can sit back down. "I don't think so . . . but try."

"Jabberwocky!" Lexie says triumphantly.

Priti laughs and even Theo smiles.

I don't like being laughed at, but if it got Theo to smile, I guess it was worth it.

"That was Alex's idea," Priti tells Lexie.

"See? I know him so well," Lexie says. "Alex is so predictable."

Priti looks at me. "Totally."

I'm glad everyone is having so much fun at my expense.

I fantasize about taking Priti's nice neat binder and spilling it over the table and saying "Ha! You didn't predict *that!*"

But I would never actually do that.

Maybe I am predictable.

Lexie looks at the outline in Priti's binder.

"So . . . here's the big question—who's going to play Alice?"

Priti looks around the lunchroom. "Who is the best actress in our class?"

"That's obvious," I say. "Persephone Chang. No contest."

"Exactly." Priti nods.

Lexie taps Priti on the shoulder. "Um . . . don't look now, but there she is."

We follow her gaze and see Persephone deep in conversation with Jojo, Joie, and Oona. They are miming their whole plot, including the injury, the fear, the ultimate victory. Persephone looks entranced. She nods, and there are squeals as all four girls hug.

"Looks like you lost your Alice," Lexie says.

CHAPTER 18

What's in a Name?

Priti marches over to Persephone and company with all of us following. We need to see how she's going to manage this. As we get closer, we can hear Jojo and the other girls in a chorus.

"You won't get hurt, 'cause I'll do all your stunts," Jojo says.

"It's sooo dramatic!" Joie adds. "You get to cry and everything!"

Oona chimes in with the final touch. "And we all get to work together! It'll be like a party!"

To my relief, Persephone doesn't look convinced. "Well . . . I mean, I was already offered the starring role in Felix's movie."

"But this is about the human spirit!" Jojo says impatiently as if that should settle everything.

"*And* you get to cry!" Joie reminds her.

Persephone has Felix's script under her arm. "Yeah, but Felix says the only films that win the Golden Reel are by members of Beaverton's class."

Priti makes her presence known. I don't know how she does it, but all eyes turn to her.

"First off, how is Jojo going to do your stunts? She's like a head taller than you."

"And she has red hair and isn't Asian," I add helpfully.

Priti shoots me a look that clearly means "Don't help." "Second, do you *like* Felix's movie idea?"

Persephone looks up at Priti. "It's . . . I mean, I like the *idea* and everything, but it's not really . . . a lot of laughs."

"Exactly!" Oona chimes in. "Ours has lots of laughs!"

"I thought yours was about a girl getting hurt on a vault."

Jojo glares at Priti. "It *still* has lots of laughs. And don't worry about the stunts. I will wear a wig and nobody's going to care that we're different heights."

"Or that you're not Asian?" I ask.

Lexie pokes me so hard I cough. "What? What?"

"Just let Priti handle this, okay?" Lexie says under her breath.

I turn to Theo, but he's vanished into thin air. I should be used to this by now. He seems more concerned about his privacy than who's going to star in our movie.

Priti leans down. "What if I told you we were doing a movie where you could sing?"

Persephone's eyes light up.

Priti always knows exactly the right thing to say.

"She can sing in our movie!" Jojo protests. "And she's my friend."

Ai-yi-yi. The friend card.

It's true that Persephone and Jojo have been best friends for most of lower and middle school. But it's also true that since Jojo started gymnastics, she hasn't been spending a lot of time with Persephone. So it's a little rich for her to pull this.

"Remember the adventures we had together?" Jojo asks.

Persephone looks torn. "I wish I could do all three."

"But you can't," Priti says matter-of-factly.

"I'm going to have to think about this," Persephone says before heading out of the lunchroom.

Jojo's eyes narrow as she turns to her teammates. "Don't worry. She's coming over to my house after school. Leave it to me."

/////

Persephone texted Priti and told her that she would let us know at assembly.

We're all gathered together, restlessly listening to the usual announcements of school trips, upcoming chorus concerts, and basketball games. Then Mrs. Hannigan turns to Felix, who is standing next to her.

"Felix has an announcement he would like to make," Mrs. Hannigan says. "Please give him your attention." She hands Felix the microphone.

I assume it's some march or boycott or something like that, so I'm a little thrown when Felix steps forward and holds up a sheaf of papers. "Thank you, Mrs. Hannigan. I'm just making a public announcement to ask if anyone has information about Mr. Harvey Konigsberg, who has been missing since yesterday, please report it to the middle school office."

He starts handing out papers to people. As they are being passed around, Felix continues. "He is a passionate believer in our cause, and no one knows what has happened to him. We have put up notices on social media and asked the police, but so far no one has any leads."

The papers are thrust into my hand by Brandon and I take one. Staring up at me is a photo of someone who I recognize well.

I look over at Lexie, who's staring at the paper in disbelief.

"So I repeat, if anyone—*anyone*—has information, it would be great for his family in the Bronx and his fellow believers in community activism if you could share it."

Lexie leans into me. "He's looking right at Adam Tolliver."

I shake my head. "That's really kind of nasty. I mean, just because it's his father's project doesn't mean Adam's dad had anything to do with this."

Priti turns to us. "I didn't realize he's one of those Tollivers. They built our building too."

"All I know about Adam is that he hit me once in gym

class and told Mr. Johnson I slipped and fell on his fist," Lexie grumbles.

I thought about the ambush at Haddad's. "If you think Adam's bad, you should meet his mother."

"So you're saying his *mom* could have had something to do with this?" Theo asks. He, as always, pops up out of nowhere.

Mrs. Hannigan is looking our way with a very ticked off look on her face. "Please give Felix your full attention."

"That's really all I wanted to say," Felix continues. "Oh wait! I also need to find another old man to be in our movie if Mr. Konigsberg doesn't show up. So if any of you have grand-parents . . ."

Boy, Felix sure has his priorities straight.

"All right, Felix," Mrs. Hannigan says, grabbing the mic. "If there are no other announcements, you may go to class."

As we are filing out, we see Persephone with Jojo and her team. Felix pushes through the crowd.

This should be good.

"Persephone! You're starring in our film, right?" Felix practically yells.

"She's changed her mind," Jojo says, looking like she just got a perfect ten for her floor routine.

"But . . . but . . . you promised!" Felix wails.

"I never promised," Persephone says.

Felix clearly sees this as yet another injustice to be bat-tled. "But I asked you first!"

"That's true," Persephone admits. "But I never committed to you."

During all this, Lexie has pulled Priti aside. She whispers something in Priti's ear.

Priti's eyes pop open and she nods excitedly. She takes out her copy of our story and crosses out a word on the first page. She and Lexie are giggling as she writes something carefully in the same place.

Persephone is clearly getting fed up with Felix. "Look, I have to get to history. I've made up my mind. I'm choosing—"

Priti shoves her copy of the script into Persephone's hands. Persephone looks down briefly.

Her whole face glows.

"I'm choosing Priti and Alex's," she announces.

Wait . . . What sorcery is this?

Jojo is not having it. "*What?* Last night you told me that you were looking forward to learning all about gymnastics."

"Things have changed," Persephone says. "And I have to get to history."

She gives Jojo a big hug and then announces, "Anyway, you *know* you'd be better in the lead role than I ever would, Jojo. You will be *amazing* in it."

Jojo turns bright red.

"She's right, actually," Joie says, hugging Jojo. "You will be *awesome.*"

"I know, right?" Oona says, as if this was the plan all along.

Persephone turns to Felix, who at this point has an entire argument lined up and ready to go.

"So since I asked you first—" Felix begins.

Persephone holds up her hand. "Firsties is so lower school.

You're better than that, Felix. And I happen to know that Jill Steenbergen is dying to play this role," she adds.

Felix looks like he's just won a victory over the forces of oppression. "The *ninth* grader? The one who played Lady Macbeth?"

"Yes!" Persephone says, wincing. "But when you ask her, remember we don't say that name because it's bad luck in the theater."

"Right!" Felix says, backing off to rush up the stairs. "What do you call it again?"

"The Scottish play!" Persephone yells after him.

She turns to Priti and grins. "I have no idea if Jill wants to play the part, but she's super nice and will probably say yes."

"Wait," I say. "So that was a lie?"

Persephone laughs. "It's called *acting*."

Priti leans down and gives her a hug. "That's our star! Come on! I'll walk you to history. I have math on the same floor."

Persephone beams. "This is going to be *epic*. I have so many ideas!"

As they practically skip up the stairs, I hear Priti say, "I cannot wait to hear them!"

I turn to Lexie. "You're pretty proud of yourself, aren't you?"

"You're welcome," Lexie snaps.

"Don't expect a hug from me," I warn.

"Don't flatter yourself, *Xan*," Lexie says, taking out a piece of gum.

We head down to our class.

"Okay, so how did you do it?" I ask.

"You mean how did I come up with the brilliant idea that got Persephone to star in *your* film, which I am not even a part of? How come I'm so smart?"

I can't stand it when she's like this. "Well, I *am* surprised," I say. "I would have thought Priti would have come up with it."

I thought Lexie would say something smart back but instead she gets quiet.

Her lower lip looks like mine does when I'm trying hard not to cry.

Now I feel like a total jerk. "I'm sorry, Lexie. That didn't come out right. I didn't mean you're not as smart as Priti."

"You totally did," Lexie says, and runs on ahead.

I catch up with her just as she's about to go into the class. "Oh, come on, at least tell me what you thought of. I mean, we both know I'm not smart enough to have thought of it."

Lexie wipes her eyes on her sleeve. "That's for sure."

She thinks for a minute, and then can't stand my not knowing her genius.

She grabs my outline and scribbles something on it.

I look down.

Alice has been crossed out. Another word has replaced it.

The title of our movie now reads: *Persephone in Anselmland*.

CHAPTER 19

Playing Games

For as long as I can remember, the first Thursday of the month has always been Game Night in the Davis household. Usually, Violet plays on Dad's team unless Mom has picked Sorry! or Candy Land.

No matter what game we play, Violet always has to win, or she will throw the mother of all tantrums, which is getting really old since she is seven years old, for crying out loud.

I have argued that it would be an important life lesson for her to learn how to be a good loser, but apparently she loses at games all the time in school and is a *wonderful* loser. So it's just us family members who get to enjoy the fireworks. Or waterworks. Or both.

Tonight it's Violet's turn to pick the game, and as always, she chooses Monopoly, which is nobody else's favorite. Dad doesn't like it because he's all, "Honey, this is just what I do at work all day."

And Mom and I hate it because Violet plays on a team with Dad, who, despite all his moaning and groaning, always manages to win, and win big. He just seems to know what properties to invest in and when to put hotels on them and stuff.

So here we are, with the stacks of money in front of Mom and me dwindling rapidly while Violet cackles like a demon counting and recounting the piles that she and Dad have acquired.

"Felix was passing out flyers about Mr. Konigsberg," I say, trying to distract Dad from buying Park Place and failing miserably.

Dad makes his purchase and looks up. "I really wish people wouldn't jump to conclusions."

This is the most my dad will ever say about a pending case.

My mom on the other hand . . .

"That was the most ridiculous stunt. Valerie Terrier should be ashamed of herself."

"What's up?" I ask. Valerie Terrier is Felix's mom.

Mom rolls the dice and lands on one of Dad's thousand hotels. She hands over all her money. "Well, I'm out."

"*Yaaay!*" screams Violet, always the gracious winner.

Mom turns to me. "That flyer. Making the whole neighborhood crazy. It's one thing to have a difference of opinion, but—"

"Allie!" Dad says sharply. "I'd love to not have to talk about this tonight."

"Alex asked a question," Mom answers. "And it's not like something really happened to him."

"Your turn!" Violet orders me. I roll the dice, and surprise, surprise! I'm on one of their properties!

Violet holds out her hand and I count out the last of my hundreds. I only have two fifties and a ten left.

"Glad this isn't real life," I say. "I guess if it was, someone would have torn down those houses and built a giant tower."

My dad snaps at me. "Alex! Enough!"

I can't remember when he'd used this tone with me before. "Dad, lighten up. I was just making a joke."

Dad starts collecting the money and putting it away.

"We're not done!" Violet protests.

"It's fine," I say. "I was gonna lose anyway."

Mom helps to gather all the pieces and puts them in the box as my dad grunts and moves to the kitchen.

Mom follows and I hear them talk in low voices.

Violet is oblivious. "I'm the winner, you're the loser!" she chants over and over.

My mom comes back in and scoops up Violet. "Time for B, B, and B, Your Highness."

B, B, and B stands for Bed Bath & Beyond (like the store)—it's a family tradition to use it whenever it's time for bedtime.

It started with me, but when Violet came along, we let her think it was made up for her.

I watch Mom carry her upstairs and try to remember what that was like. It seems so long ago. Sometimes I wish Dad or Mom could scoop me up and carry me to bed again, but of course that's silly. Even when I'm sick or something, my dad says, "You're too big to carry," and I have to drag my sorry butt upstairs all by myself.

Dad sits next to me on the couch. "Alex, I shouldn't have yelled at you like that. I apologize."

I laugh. "Dad, you weren't yelling. But thanks anyway."

He puts his arm around me, and I smell his aftershave, which reminds me of when he used to read to me every night, with me snuggled in his arm, turning the pages.

"So, Mr. Konigsberg," my dad begins. "Here's the thing. He was visiting his daughter up in Vermont. And he doesn't have a cell phone."

"He didn't tell anyone he was going?" I ask, thinking of his roommate, Mr. Birnbaum.

"He might have mentioned it, but the man he lives with doesn't remember so well."

I sigh and settle back into my dad's chest. "So he's fine."

"Yes, he'll be back screaming at me tomorrow, no doubt," Dad says.

I shake my head. "I know Mr. Konigsberg was thrown out of his apartment, but that wasn't even Mr. Tolliver's building. I don't see how that gives him the right—"

My dad sits up and stares me full in the face. "Alex, never

say that. He has every right to do what he's doing. Protesting and speaking your mind are some of the most important things that make us Americans. Think of all the good that's come of people protesting."

Now I'm confused. "So you think they're right."

"It doesn't matter if they're right or not. It's their right. Even their right to be wrong."

Dad laughs at his own corny joke.

"So you think they're wrong," I press him.

Dad thinks for a minute. "I honestly don't know who's right and who's wrong. That's why this hearing is important. It allows us to hear both sides of the argument."

"Bill!" my mother calls from upstairs. "Violet is requesting Elephant and Piggie."

We both know what that means. Mom can't do the voices the way Dad does them, so he's being called to service.

"It's okay, I need to write some scenes for the movie," I tell him as he kisses me on the cheek.

"Oh! You haven't been talking about that," my dad says. "How's it going?"

I'm glad I don't have to lie. "Really, really well. We got Persephone Chang to star in it as Alice."

My dad looks confused. "Dad. You saw her last year in *Annie*, remember?" I remind him.

"Right. The teeny girl with the big voice," he says. "That's great."

I nod, and he heads upstairs.

I am about to get up when I turn my head and realize that our school directory is on the bookshelf directly behind me.

The one with every parent in the school in it.

And their addresses. And phone numbers.

I pull it out and start to thumb through it.

I pass the names of movie stars, famous novelists, journalists, and some kids I recognize from my class. I run my finger down the page until I get to "Schatten."

The listing says: *Schatten, Theodore. Parents, Dare Young & Immie Schatten. Address, email, and telephone: not provided.*

My first reaction is of course Theo's parents would have *interesting* names. And the second is that the only other person to not give their information listed is Matthew Abbott and he is, well, *Matthew Abbott.* When your films gross over five billion dollars, I guess you get some privacy. But even he had an email for his contact. (I know this because Noel tried to contact him with a *brilliant* idea for a movie and got back a polite response from Mr. Abbott's assistant.)

I'm pretty sure D. Young Schatten isn't a world-famous actor. Or director.

I try to find Theo's dad or mom online.

The closest I can find is a company called "Schatten InfoSec," but when I go to the site, it requires a password to even view the home page.

Yeah, that sounds like Theo.

CHAPTER 20

The Boy in the Yearbook

Priti and I have a free period before film class, so we decide to get together in the library and figure out who we are going to ask to play what roles.

Theo has a chem class, so he can't join us. He's totally cool with us doing this, since he's only been here a little while and doesn't really know everyone like us old-timers do.

I usually come to the library to do homework or fool around on the school computers. You're not supposed to play games on them, but let's be real . . . some kids do. I'm not saying I'm one of them; I just know some who do.

Okay, maybe I do after I've finished my homework. Or need a break. Sorry.

Anyhow, I haven't seen Priti in the library all semester,

even though she has a free period. She's probably hanging out with Jensen. I mean, why wouldn't she be?

I spot Priti at the large wood-paneled entrance. She hesitates. I wave at her, but she isn't looking my way.

I follow her gaze and realize why she hasn't been in the library this year.

On the wall is a newly hung portrait of Isabel Archer's mother, who was the librarian here forever. It's a beautiful oil painting and looks just like her. She's seated at one of the tables, in her signature blue cardigan (she must have had a closetful of them), looking out at the viewer, as if to say, "Well, Alex!" (She knew all our names). "What will it be today?" I can see they have put some of her favorite books on the table around her, from *The 13 Clocks* and *The Phantom Tollbooth* to *Charlotte's Web* and *Anne of Green Gables.*

Priti was really close to her, going on ski trips with Isabel (we'd hear all about it in class), so when she died last year, I guess it hit her really hard.

It's understandable she wouldn't want to come here.

I walk over to her. "We don't have to meet here."

Priti turns her gaze to me. Her eyes are clear. "No, I really need to get over this. I'm being silly."

"I don't think you're being silly," I say. "You really loved Mrs. Archer."

Priti sighs. "I guess I did. I really did."

She marches over to an empty table by the window. Light is streaming in, that early October light that's still strong in the morning.

"So! Any ideas?" she asks, taking out her binder.

She's printed out a complete character sheet, and we get to work filling it in with the names of our first choices. Some of them will probably be in other films, and others, like the director of the school, will be too busy.

Then again, it's hard to say no to Priti Sharma.

We just have a few more roles to fill when Lexie runs up to the table. She's all out of breath.

"I've been looking for you guys everywhere!" she pants.

"What's up?" I ask.

Lexie wipes her face with her T-shirt. I'm not sure, but I think I see Priti wince.

Lexie's eyes are shining. "So I was in the office, and you are *never* going to guess what I found!"

I decide to torture her.

"What were you doing in the office?"

"It doesn't matter," Lexie says. "But I found out—"

"You weren't sick, right? Because then you'd go to the nurse."

"No, I'm not sick. Anyway—"

"Were you there to see Mrs. Hannigan?"

"That's not the point!" Lexie screams, earning a loud "Lexie, *please*" from Mrs. Falatko, the new librarian.

Lexie glares at me.

"Don't mind him," Priti says. "He's just being a jerk."

"As usual," Lexie mutters. She turns to me. "May I please tell my story?"

"Who's stopping you?" I ask with a smirk.

I have had years of practice torturing my little sister.

Lexie looks right at Priti. "So while I was waiting for my . . . thing . . . I noticed they have a bookcase in there with all the yearbooks going back to the first years of the school. So I started looking through them."

"And you found something for our movie?"

Lexie stops for a moment. "Did you ever notice how Theo just kind of appears and disappears?"

"Hard not to," I answer.

"And how he won't ever say where he's from . . . and how he's really pale?" Lexie is practically whispering now.

Priti is fidgeting with her pen. "Yes. Of course."

Lexie leans all the way in. "So . . . I was looking in a yearbook from fifty years ago. It was pretty wild, seeing all those seventies clothes and stuff. Anyhow, who do you think the yearbook is dedicated to?"

"I have no idea," I say.

"One Theo Schatten, who died that year. He had been in a car crash." Lexie's eyes dart back and forth between us. "Huh? *Huh?* Creepy, right?"

Priti is not impressed. "Lexie, really. Theo is probably just named after him. Like he was his uncle or something."

"There is a photo. Long hair, pale oval face. It's him," Lexie says firmly.

A bead of cold sweat runs down the back of my T-shirt. "That's impossible."

"Is it?" Lexie asks. "What do we really know about him?"

Priti and I lean back, silent, trying to process this.

"Wow," Priti finally says.

Lexie can't take it any longer. She explodes in laughter. "*Psych!* I *cannot* believe you guys actually went for that!"

"You are a total butt," I say.

"You should have seen your faces!" Lexie crows, getting a very ticked off *"Shhh!"* from Mrs. Falatko.

"I never believed it." Priti sniffs.

"You totally did," Lexie says. "Admit it."

Priti gives a shy smile. "Okay, maybe for a *second* I considered it, but it doesn't make sense logically. I mean, Beaverton has been here like fifty years and would have remembered something like that."

Lexie smacks the side of her head. "Oh yeah! I forgot that. Oh well, Alex was all in."

"Considering his parents don't even have their information in the parents' guide, it certainly didn't seem out of the question," I say.

Priti looks at me with what I think is admiration. "Nice one, Alex. I didn't think to check that. That is strange. Especially since he made it his business to know what all *our* parents do." She turns to Lexie. "Well, you certainly pulled that off. You're quite the little actress!"

Lexie actually blushes. "I suppose I am."

Priti flashes a triumphant smile. "Good! So you'll be perfect as the Mock Turtle!" Priti writes Lexie's name on the form.

"Wait a minute!" Lexie says. "I didn't agree to this! I can't act!"

Now it's my turn for revenge. "You just did. That was your audition."

Before Lexie can protest any more, Priti closes her binder. "You're doing it, Lexie, and you'll be great. I'm sure Alex has written a hilarious scene for you."

Oh, right, I had forgotten that the Mock Turtle's poem was one of my assignments.

Lexie's shoulders slump. "Oh, *great*."

"Hey!" I say. "How do you know it won't be good?"

Priti pats Lexie on the shoulder. "Don't worry, if it stinks, I'll just make it better."

Lexie brightens. "Oh, in that case, I'm cool with it."

CHAPTER 21

Pablo Likes His Stakes Well Done

We still have a few minutes before class, and Lexie and Priti are talking about some girl on Instagram they are both obsessed with (I didn't even know Lexie went on those apps, but she seems to have a deep well of knowledge about the current scandal about this person, which is simply riveting), so I gather up my things.

"I think I'll go up early," I announce with absolutely no one paying attention or caring.

I head up to the ninth floor and the door is already open.

I walk in to find Pablo in a heated discussion with Mr. Beaverton.

I always hate it in those books I read where the main

character "just *happens*" to walk by a door or is hiding under a table (looking at you, Harry Potter) just as the most important information to the plot is being discussed. Like, wow, what a coincidence!

So it would have been great if I'd just stood outside the door and listened in on the conversation and overheard something really damaging about Mr. Beaverton, like that the real reason he hates our team is because Theo is really his nephew and he has always hated Theo's father because he stole the love of his life. You know, something like that.

But instead, like a boob, I just barge in and they stop talking. Then Pablo checks his watch and says, "Um, Alex, would you mind waiting outside until the bell rings?"

I take my bag and head out. "Sure thing!"

"And close the door behind you," he adds.

Beaverton of course doesn't even acknowledge my existence.

I leave and can't help it. I park myself right by the door and try to make out what they are saying. It's not hard, since they're . . . Let's say they're not using their indoor voices.

"Pablo, this is so unlike you. Art for art's sake and all that."

"I want my kids to make their best films. If they win, so be it."

"Oh, they won't. I'm even willing to bet on it."

"If you were so sure, you wouldn't have pulled that stunt with Priti Sharma."

"I was misinformed. But don't worry, Felix has this in the bag."

"I don't think so. And I think you know that too."

There is a nasty laugh. Clearly Mr. Beaverton. I cannot imagine it coming from Pablo.

"Laugh all you want. We'll see who's laughing when one of my kids wins the Golden Reel this year."

"Oh, let's look at your class, shall we? A prank war? A bunch of girl gymnasts jumping around? Some kids waving swords at each other? And some movie that's filled with inside jokes about the school that Hannah and Cody aren't going to find amusing. Satire only works if you know what it is that's being made fun of. I guess you weren't paying attention when I taught that in class. But then again, you were never the best student."

Pablo mutters something I can't hear.

"I'm sorry, what was that?" Beaverton asks. Luckily he couldn't hear it either.

"I said at least I don't write my students' scripts for them."

"We both know that's a lie, but if it makes you feel better, then believe what you want."

"We both know it's the truth," Pablo says. "And you do your students no favors when you don't let them make their own mistakes."

"I don't think Hannah and Cody have done all that badly."

The first bell rings.

"We'll continue this another time, Pablo."

"Just remember how that stunt with Jensen's brother ended up. Stay away from my students. Let them fail or succeed on their own."

There is movement inside and I jump back from the door, bumping into Theo, who is right behind me.

I stifle a yell. "Jeez, Theo, warn a person. How long have you been back there?"

Theo grins. "Since pretty much right after you got here. I guess I'm not the only one who likes to eavesdrop, huh?"

I am about to answer when I'm hit in the face with a Nerf dart.

"Think quick!" Nathan says, brandishing his Nerf gun.

"You're supposed to say that *before* you shoot someone," I grouse.

Nathan cocks the mechanism. "Oh, right. I always forget that."

He aims at Jojo, who is coming up to us along with the other kids filing into the room.

"I wouldn't," I warn.

Jojo sees the Nerf gun and wrestles it away from Nathan. She then shoots at him like eight times.

Nathan crouches into a ball, defeated, as the foam darts rain down on him.

"Can I have that back?" Nathan pleads. "It's a prop for our movie."

Jojo looks down on her vanquished foe. "Don't ever mess with me again, Nathan. I will destroy you. And no, you can't have it."

She strides onward and drops the Nerf gun onto Pablo's desk as she passes.

Jojo is quite the competitor, I decide. The type who will do anything to win.

I go in and take my seat next to Priti. Since today is a work-day, Theo noiselessly appears at the desk on her other side.

Pablo takes his place in the front of the room. He claps his hands and we quiet down.

"Today is the first day to work on our actual scripts. Please remember that when we talk about our collaborators' work, we are going to be supportive and constructive."

We pass each other copies of our scenes.

I look at Theo's first. He was doing the Cheshire cat scene.

INT. MIDDLE SCHOOL OFFICE—DAY

Persephone sees Mrs. Whitman sitting on her desk, grinning. She is wearing cat ears.

PERSEPHONE
Would you tell me, please, which way I ought to go from here?

WHITMAN CAT
That depends a good deal on where you want to get to.

PERSEPHONE

I don't much care where.

WHITMAN CAT

Then it doesn't matter which way
you go.

PERSEPHONE

—so long as I get *somewhere*.

WHITMAN CAT

Oh, you're sure to do that. If you
only walk long enough.

PERSEPHONE

What sort of people live about here?

WHITMAN CAT

In *that* direction is the faculty
lounge, and in *that* direction is
the high school student lounge.
Visit either you like: they're
both mad.

PERSEPHONE

But I don't want to go among mad
people.

                        WHITMAN CAT

    Then you're at the wrong school.
    We're all mad here. I'm mad.
    You're mad.

                        PERSEPHONE

    How do you know I'm mad?

                        WHITMAN CAT

    You must be—or you wouldn't have
    come here.

WHITMAN CAT grins and vanishes.

Theo is chewing on his nail. "So . . . what do you guys think?"

"Well, I mean . . . all you did basically was copy and paste from the original, right?" I ask.

"I added a *lot*," Theo insists. "I changed it from Cheshire cat to Whitman cat."

Priti writes a few notes on the side of the page. "I think *mad* should be changed to *crazy*. *Mad* sounds like *angry*."

"But in England it means crazy," Theo insists.

"But we're not in England," I say.

Theo crosses his arms in front of him. "You get it from the context."

"Theo, it's just bad this way," Priti says.

I guess we didn't realize how loud we were talking, because Pablo comes over to our area. "Guys. Settle down. It sounds like you're having what we call *creative differences*."

Priti thrusts Theo's pages into his hands. "You could say that."

Pablo scans them. "So what's the issue?"

"First of all," I say, "he just took the lines right out of the book."

Pablo looks over at Theo and nods. "But he's put them in the context of Saint Anselm's. The fact that they work so well and are the actual text from the original is pretty clever if you ask me."

"Okay," Priti says. "But I want to change the word *mad* to *crazy*. His way is just bad."

Pablo winces. "Um . . . can you think of a more constructive way to say that?"

Priti thinks for a second. "I guess . . . it could be worse?"

"How about . . . even though you're technically right, Theo, it's less confusing to our audience to use the word *crazy*," I say.

Pablo brightens. "There! What do you think, Theo?"

"I think it's dumb, but I don't mind changing it," Theo says, crossing out the words on his script.

"Excellent! Now we're getting somewhere," Pablo exclaims.

"Take that, Mr. Beaverton!" I add, which I thought would make Pablo smile.

Instead, it seems to remind him of something.

Pablo goes to the front of the room and claps again. "Listen,

163

I don't want to interrupt anyone's creative flow, but there's something I need you to focus on as you write your scenes. I need you to ask yourself, what are the stakes? Are they high enough? Are we going to care about your characters?"

He turns to Nathan and Mateo. "For example, what are the stakes in your movie?"

They look like he's just asked them to define a quadratic equation.

"Umm . . . not to get hit so many times in the groin?" Nathan suggests.

Pablo nods. "Okay . . . and?"

"And to be funny?" Mateo adds.

"I need more than that!" Pablo says, suddenly seeming very Beavertonish.

"To win the prank war!" Noel says, always with the answers.

Pablo turns on Noel. "That's just a plot. There's nothing at stake. Haven't I taught you kids anything?"

We're all a little stunned.

"How about if they like the same girl? And they're trying to impress her?" Pablo suggests. "That would be good, right?"

Nathan makes a face. "No offense, but that's kind of corny."

"Just try it," Pablo says.

Pablo turns to Jojo and her crew. "How about you?"

"Well, the stakes are pretty high, don't you think? Like overcoming your fear?" Jojo says.

Pablo looks unimpressed. "I need more. Like if she doesn't

make the vault, she loses her scholarship and her chances of going to a good college are ruined."

"But that's ridiculous," Oona says. "We're in middle school. This isn't going to count toward college. And it's unrealistic anyway."

"I don't care if it's realistic," Pablo says. "Part of making movies is adding drama to real situations. Do you think any of those movies 'based on real events' are realistic? They always add things."

"I think it's enough that she doesn't want to let her team down," Joie says.

"All right, but it should be the tryouts for the Olympics," Pablo says.

Jojo laughs. "That's really too far."

Ignoring her, Pablo turns to Noel and RPG. Cammi, shy as ever, is cowering behind them. "How about you guys?"

"Our heroes have to save the world! If the villain gets a hold of the scepter of power, he will be unbeatable!" RPG exclaims.

Pablo nods. "Not bad. But what if it turns out he's not the real villain?"

"We can't put that in! It's hard enough doing all this in a ten-minute movie!" Noel protests.

"If it will make it better, you can find a way."

Now it's our turn.

Pablo looks at us.

I try to come up with something that will make him happy.

"Well, it's about the changes Saint Anselm's has to make in order to—"

Priti stops me. "Pablo. Shouldn't you let us write our own movies?"

The silence in the room is so total you can hear the traffic in the street below. A car horn blares. There is a baby crying in a stroller. I hear kids laughing in the hallway.

Finally Pablo's whole body seems to slump. He takes off his glasses. There is a small smile on his lips like he's having a private joke with himself. He shakes his head as he walks back to his desk. He doesn't turn around when he speaks to us.

"Thank you, Priti," he says. "Kids, forget everything I said. You write your own movies. And they will be either good or bad. But they will be yours."

CHAPTER 22

Democracy in Action, aka a Lot of Grown-Ups Yelling

Not gonna lie, this collaborative writing stuff is not easy. We send scenes back and forth, and half the time I think Priti's changes are dumb and the other half she thinks my jokes are garbage. Theo doesn't seem to care one way or another, at least.

Whenever we get stuck, Pablo acts as a referee, but honestly, what comes out as a compromise usually means he takes Priti's side. She would probably tell you otherwise. But we finally have something that we're all happy with. Kinda.

"So when do I get to read it?" Lexie asks.

I laugh. "Other than your scene? Like, never."

Lexie sniffs. "I wasn't asking you. I was asking Priti."

"If it gets boring in there, I'll let you read my copy," Priti says.

The entire seventh grade is walking over to the big civil administration building on Adams Street, which is right across from the school.

We are going to the preliminary hearing for the Court Street Towers Project.

Neighborhood individuals and groups are allowed to ask questions of the developer (that would be Mr. Tolliver) and the Building Commission, which of course includes my dad. The idea is that this is kind of a civics lesson, since we're covering the American government system in history right now.

Priti is hanging out with us, which I am a little surprised by. Lunch is one thing, but this is a school trip. I think the cool girls are getting a little weirded out, but we all know it's going to end after the film project is over. But for now she spends more time with us, and I'm happy that she and Lexie seem to have grown tight, considering how different they are.

I see Felix with a few other kids from our class who are as passionately antidevelopment as he is. They are all carrying signs that they plan to hold up during the hearing. Felix also has a camera bag from Saint Anselm's slung over his shoulder.

Priti glares at him. "I cannot believe he got permission to shoot footage of the meeting to use in his film."

"That's impossible," I say. "They never let the press shoot during the session."

Priti steps aside as Felix pushes past her, dodging the

swinging camera bag. "I got this from Noel, who seems to know everything. He's allowed to shoot footage before and after and he's going to intercut scenes with his actors."

"How'd he get that?" Lexie asks.

"Believe it or not, the councilman is an ex-student of Beaverton's," Priti says flatly.

"Why am I not surprised?" I mutter.

We wait for the light to change as the imposing gray slab of the Civic Administration Building of Kings County, Brooklyn, looms up ahead.

We enter the building and go through the metal detector, which takes forever. Then we go up the echoing marble stairs to a room with plastic seats from like the seventies that have indentations for your butt that never feel comfortable.

Did people from the seventies have smaller butts?

There are a bunch of seats in the front taped off with Saint Anselm's printed on paper sheets on each one.

I see my dad and wave. He's on a stage next to the podium, where he's having a conversation with the commissioner, Dan Rubin. I assume Mr. Rubin will be running the meeting.

There is a team of people setting up a little model of a skyscraper on a table near the stage and a screen behind it. They're all dressed better than anyone else in the room. A guy in shirtsleeves who seems to be Dad's age is directing them. Even with his back to us, you can tell he's the kind of person who goes to the gym a *lot*. When he turns around, it's clear he's Adam's dad. He's got a shaved head and fancy-looking glasses.

There is a lot of noise in the room as people take their seats. An older woman with a silk scarf around her neck complains loudly that we kids have been given all the good seats, which is weird because she's sitting like right across from us in the same row.

I guess some people like to complain.

Mr. Rubin leans into the microphone. "Please take your seats so the meeting can begin."

He has a strong New York accent, which makes him sound impatient even when he isn't. He consults some notes on the podium. "The meeting will come to order. This is how things are going to go. First, Tolliver Development will make their presentation. Then we will entertain questions from the audience. Please do not yell out your questions. There are cards on your seats. Put your question on that card and we will collect them and read them from the podium, as per the rules of the commission."

There's a small commotion at the front of the room. A youngish man in a suit and tie enters and sits on the opposite end of the table as my dad.

"Who's that?" Lexie asks.

I don't answer.

Lexie pokes me in the ribs. "I asked you a question."

"I thought you weren't asking me. You were asking Priti," I say.

"You can be such a butt sometimes," Lexie grumbles.

I decide to be nice. "He's our councilman, Derek Randolph.

He represents our district in the city council. He has to give the final approval. He hasn't said which way he'll vote."

Lexie shakes her head. "It's so weird to think of him taking film class with Beaverton."

Priti has been hard at work on our script this whole time. She's crossing out entire lines from the scene I gave her right before we got here. I watch as she writes a giant *?* next to one of my favorite jokes in the whole movie.

She may be smart and beautiful, but at this moment I hate her *so much*.

Mr. Rubin looks a little annoyed at Mr. Randolph's late entrance. "Glad to see you could make it, Councilman."

Derek Randolph is looking down at his phone and absent-mindedly nods. He peers out into the assembled audience and sees Mr. Beaverton and waves.

Mr. Beaverton gives him a small bow. I bet he volunteered to be a teacher/chaperone just so everyone could see what a big shot he is.

I look over at my dad, who has a yellow legal pad and three pens in front of him. Three, because one might not work, and then the other might run out of ink before the meeting is over.

That's my dad.

Mr. Rubin clears his throat. "I now turn the meeting over to Mr. Calvin Tolliver, the president of Tolliver Development."

Mr. Tolliver jumps into action.

He starts by showing a short video about the project.

It's really well done, with lots of pictures of smiling New

Yorkers from all backgrounds. There are young families push-ing strollers, old couples holding hands, kids on bikes. All ac-companied by soothing music.

And above it all, gleaming like a jewel, is Court Street Towers.

There is a voice-over, deep and reassuring, with words like *positive community impact* and how "the existing neighbor-hood will not be affected."

Which is a nice way of saying that *No Konigsbergs will be harmed in the making of this building.*

Priti leans in and whispers, "Is it me or does it remind you of a commercial for a drug company?"

Lexie giggles. "I know, right? I expect to hear the voice-over say 'Side effects may include . . . '"

She gets a very loud "SHH!" from the lady across the aisle.

I think it's nice. I turn to Theo, who is slumped in his seat. He has his hair in front of his face. I decide now is not the time to ask him anything.

After the film is over, the lights come back up and Mr. Tol-liver has a slide presentation. Point by point, it seems to take on all the concerns of the community. He shows how local businesses have been suffering, and this project will bring much-needed new people into the neighborhood. How as part of their agreement with the city, Tolliver will be convert-ing a nearby abandoned warehouse into affordable housing for a hundred people.

He shows all sorts of charts with titles like ENVIRONMEN-TAL IMPACT STUDY and LISTENING TO OUR NEIGHBORS.

When he's done, part of the room erupts in applause and another part of the room boos. Some of my dad's interns are accepting cards from the audience and bringing them up to Commissioner Rubin. A security guard waves at Felix and gestures for him to put away the camera.

Commissioner Rubin turns on the microphone at the podium. "And now we will be reading the questions you submitted."

He starts with the questions asking about the changing character of the neighborhood. And asks why, if Mr. Tolliver is so keen on buildings like Court Street Towers, he lives in a small town house instead of one of his own properties.

Mr. Tolliver doesn't look flustered at all. He clearly has a whole answer already prepared. He talks about how the Court Street area is a business district and has never had residences, how there are already a dozen other buildings just like his, so it wouldn't change much. He just might move into Court Street Towers if it gets built.

"I just saw the drawings for the gym and indoor pool!" he exclaims.

I turn to Priti. "He's really good."

She nods. "It's like he knows all the things they're going to ask beforehand."

There is a snort from the slumped figure next to me. "It's classic opsec."

We turn and stare at Theo.

"What's opsec?" Lexie asks.

"Operations security. Originally used in the military to

identify and protect vulnerable areas. Now, any smart business does it. There are five steps. First, identify critical information, then identify the threat, assess the project's vulnerabilities, analyze the risk, and finally develop and apply countermeasures."

Even Priti looks impressed. "Is this what your dad does?"

Theo is about to answer, then catches himself. "Nice try."

Mr. Tolliver has been answering a question about whether there will be ramps and wheelchair-accessible entries throughout the building. He looks insulted at the insinuation that they wouldn't include that.

"It wasn't in the original blueprints!" the lady who shushed us yells out. "You only added it after the Heights Housing League brought it to your attention."

Mr. Tolliver turns to her. "I don't know where you heard that, but it's not true."

"It is true," the woman insists. "I'm the chairman of that organization. Perhaps you have forgotten our meeting."

"Of course I haven't forgotten it, Mrs. Hayes," Mr. Tolliver says. "Who could forget your charming face?"

There is a ripple of laughter throughout the room.

Mrs. Hayes tries to suppress a smile. "Never mind the sweet talk, Mr. Tolliver."

Mr. Tolliver turns to the audience. "As I told Mrs. Hayes at the time, those were the most preliminary of renderings. We always add access ramps and other ADA compliance needs later in the process."

Priti turns to me. "ADA stands for the Americans with Disabilities Act."

I know she's just trying to be helpful, but really?

"I actually knew that," I say. "Considering my dad is the freaking *deputy buildings commissioner!*"

I guess I said this a little louder than I should have because my dad shoots me a dirty look.

"I didn't know it," Lexie whispers to Priti. "Thanks."

Priti leans in to Lexie. "I did a paper on it for history last year; that's how I know."

Mr. Rubin reads the next question. "Will you be using local labor and buying whenever possible from local vendors?"

Just like Theo said, Mr. Tolliver has an answer all ready to go. Every one of his buildings has made a point of hiring local workmen whenever possible, giving priority to people of color and those who otherwise are usually kept from work in the construction field.

There is real applause for this.

Even Councilman Randolph looks up from his phone. I guess he just assumes the applause was for him.

Just as Commissioner Rubin is about to ask the next question, a voice yells out from the back.

"What about the bribery?"

We all turn and see Mr. Konigsberg, a pile of papers under one arm. He's waving with the other.

Commissioner Rubin sighs. "Please, we are not taking questions from the audience."

"I demand to know about the bribes this rat Tolliver is giving Councilman Randolph!" Mr. Konigsberg shouts.

My dad stands up. "Mr. Konigsberg, please. You know we only read questions from the dais."

Commissioner Rubin turns to my dad. "You know this man?"

My dad nods. "He's a very . . . passionate member of the community."

"Answer my question! Or are you afraid of the truth?" Mr. Konigsberg proclaims as the security guards march over to him.

That seems to be a cue. A bunch of people, including Felix with his sign, stand up and start chanting, "Answer him! Answer him!"

Commissioner Rubin holds his hands up and asks for quiet. "Please! People! Be civil!"

Mr. Tolliver looks at his people.

They weren't expecting this.

The security guards are escorting Mr. Konigsberg out of the hall. He drops his papers and they scatter everywhere.

"Where are we living? Stalinist Russia?" he calls out. "You can't hide from the truth!"

There is general chaos at this point, as half the room is now chanting, "You can't hide from the truth!"

Pablo and Mr. Beaverton are trying to usher us out of the room.

As we get into the hallway, we still hear Mr. Rubin on the microphone pleading for people to return to their seats or else he will adjourn the meeting.

"That's what happens when you don't have good opsec," Theo says, nodding.

As we head onto the street, Priti turns to me. "The reason he said Stalinist Russia has to do with how dissent was treated when Joseph Stalin ran the Soviet Union. He threw people in jail or killed them."

Why am I not surprised that she feels the need to enlighten us?

I don't say anything. I just walk to the corner. Lexie catches up to me.

"What are you thinking?" Lexie asks.

I am thinking of a jail where they throw know-it-alls and weird people who know obscure information.

"Nothing," I say. "Just waiting for the light to change."

CHAPTER 23

The Most Unkindest Cut of All

As we settle into our usual seats in Film Studies, I feel calm and filled with the kind of confidence you have when you know you studied your butt off and mastered all the material covered in the test you're about to take.

Because today is the day we get Pablo's notes on our final scripts before we're given the green light to shoot it.

Mr. Beaverton likes to do it in private, so only he and the students involved hear the notes (some of us suspect that it's really because that's where he rewrites the scripts of his favorites and doesn't want other people to hear. I'm not saying that really happens, but . . . I'm not saying it *doesn't*).

Pablo, on the other hand, feels we all can learn from one another's mistakes. And looking around the room, I can't wait. Especially since our script is so good that he's no doubt going to say, "Priti, Alex, Theo . . . you're good to go. I cannot see *anything* to change here."

First, Pablo turns to Nathan and Mateo. "Really good job, guys. Adding the competition element really upped the stakes and gives us someone to root for."

Nathan and Mateo high-five.

Pablo consults his page of notes. "Yeah, there's just one thing. The curse words have to go."

Nathan looks like Pablo has asked him to cut off his arm, or another part of his body. "But . . ."

"No buts," Pablo says.

"How about butt cracks?" Mateo asks. I think he's actually serious, but everyone laughs like it's a joke.

Pablo looks up from his page. "First off, the school would fire me if I let you use these words in a film."

"It's not fair," Nathan says. "I mean, we curse all the time with our friends."

"Okay, but do you curse in front of your parents? Or your teachers?" Pablo asks.

Mateo shifts uncomfortably in his seat. "No. I guess not."

"So who do you think is going to be there watching your film?" Pablo asks. "Look, if you want to make a film with curse words, do it and put it up on YouTube. I know there's thousands of them. But just not in my class."

"It's just funnier with the curse words," Nathan protests.

"That's my second point," Pablo says. "If something is only funny because there are curses in it, maybe you need to work a little harder. There's plenty of comedy here without the cursing. Let's try and find the humor without them, okay?"

That last part was less of a question and more of a statement.

Pablo turns to Jojo and Joie and Oona. "Now, you have a great start here. But you have to remember that not everyone who is seeing your film is as intimately involved in gymnastics as you are. Some of these terms you'll need to explain to a regular audience." He reads off their script. "'Jennifer, I know you'll kill it when you make a round-off entry onto the board, flic-flac onto the vaulting table, and salto off the vaulting table.'"

"But that just means—" Jojo breaks in.

"Don't tell me, tell the audience. Also, I'm a little concerned about when she takes her fall. I want to make sure your coach is there to assure me that it's safe and no one is going to get hurt."

The three girls nod, and he moves onto RPG, Noel, and Cammi. "Guys, guys, guys . . ."

He holds up their script. It looks like it's a hundred pages. "Have you read this out loud? Do you know how long it's going to be?"

"We have a lot of story to tell," RPG says, pushing his glasses up his nose. "In order to understand why this object is so powerful, we need to give the history of how it was made, right?"

Pablo makes a face. "This would be like an hour and a half.

We're making ten-minute movies, remember? What's more, there are a lot of special effects in here," he continues, glancing at their story.

"That's the great part," Noel says confidently. "RPG's dad is going to help us with that."

Pablo shakes his head. "Nope. Noel, you know better. No parents' help. This is *your* movie."

"But in big fantasy movies, there's always a special effects department!" RPG wails. "It's still our story."

"Here's the thing," Pablo says, turning to the whole class. "Even if you never make another movie, if you're writing a novel or a play or doing anything creative, you're going to get notes from *someone*. Some you'll agree with, some you won't. I'm here to give you a taste of what that's going to be like. And you can either think creatively and approach these things as challenges rather than obstacles, or you can be stubborn and stick to your guns and not learn from other people's viewpoints. Your choice."

"So does that mean it's our choice whether we curse in our movie?" Mateo asks hopefully.

"No, Mateo. I meant it's your choice in the *future*."

"Oh, f—"

"Mateo!" Pablo says sharply.

"What? I was going to say forget about it," Mateo says innocently.

Nathan snickers as Pablo turns back to RPG and Cammi and Noel.

Ralph and Cammi have been thumbing through their

script. Ralph looks close to tears. "It can't be done," he manages to get out. "There's no way we can tell the story in ten minutes."

Suddenly, a little voice pipes up. "What if we just do part of our script? Like one of the stories? The one with the woman warrior fighting the dragon?"

At first, none of us know who's talking, because we've so rarely heard Cammi's voice.

Cammi usually doesn't talk in class, as he kind of has social anxiety, and we just accept that it's harder for him to contribute. He's been like that as long as we've known him. But that doesn't mean he isn't smart. I bet some of the best ideas came from him.

Pablo nods enthusiastically. "That's a *terrific* solution, Cammi. It looks like that scene is the perfect length and it works as a little film all in itself."

Noel looks at Ralph. "Maybe we can shoot the rest of it this summer! With your dad's equipment!"

That crisis averted, Pablo turns to us. "Now we take our trip to Wonderland."

He pulls out a copy of our masterpiece. I notice immediately that there are lines drawn through entire speeches and notes scribbled in the margins on every page.

Priti has stiffened next to me and uncapped her purple pen. Clearly she is not used to getting anything less than excellent reports.

I'm not exactly thrilled either.

"Let me start by saying that it's no help to you to tell you what's *working,*" Pablo says. "Because a lot of it is really clever and smart and has the potential to make an amazing film."

That's not so bad!

Pablo continues. "So instead, let's focus on what's *not* working, and make it better. And of course which parts have to be cut immediately, like the Caterpillar scene."

Priti and I exchange confused glances.

"But that's a really funny scene," I say.

"And more importantly, it's true," Priti adds.

Pablo looks at us like we're from another planet. "A scene with a senior *vaping*? Did you think I'd allow that?"

"He's coughing throughout the scene, right?" I try to explain. "We're showing how bad vaping is."

"It doesn't matter," Pablo says firmly. "Some of the younger kids who see this are just going to see a cool senior vaping. That's what they're going to take away from it."

"You don't know that!" Priti protests.

"We're not taking that chance. And it's in the beginning of the movie. All you need is for some of the parents to think the film is promoting vaping . . ."

"You mean all *you* need," Theo says under his breath.

Pablo takes a step toward us. "What was that, Theo?"

"Nothing," Theo says, smiling.

"Then I'm going to go on."

And he does.

For *twenty minutes*.

Every scene is cut, and at least half my favorite jokes are taken out. We fight to keep a bunch in, and Pablo begrudgingly allows a few to be filmed, with the understanding that if he or any other faculty member has a problem, they will take it out.

At long last, the ordeal is over. Or so we think.

"One more thing," Pablo says. "You have to take out the character of the Beaver."

Theo leans over his desk. "No."

Um, what?

Priti tries damage control. "What Theo means is we'll definitely work on that . . ."

"I meant no," Theo says firmly. "You've pretty much taken out everything that makes it good satire. It's like we can't say anything bad about your precious school. But the Beaver stays."

The rest of the class is dead silent, with what feels like everyone holding their breath.

Pablo is a totally cool teacher, but Theo is pushing back a little hard.

Pablo consults his script. "Theo, that's a pretty strong slam. I've left in at least fifty percent of your stuff. What I am doing is removing the parts that will be distracting to your audience."

"What's distracting about the Beaver?" Theo asks. And I think he really doesn't know.

We've never seen Pablo get mad at anyone (even Nathan and Mateo, who he just gets exasperated with), so this is new. "Theo, you've got to be kidding me. Let's start with the fact that there's no beaver in *Alice in Wonderland*—"

Priti can't help herself. "Actually, there is a beaver in the poem 'The Hunting of the Snark,' which is why we thought it was funny to make him snarky."

"Oh *please*," Pablo says in a "don't try and snow me" voice. "The Beaver is clearly supposed to be a caricature of Mr. Beaverton. That's the only reason he's there."

The class titters.

"Dang," Mateo says in the corner. "That's pretty harsh."

"And what if it is?" Theo challenges. "Are you afraid of him? Why can't we make a caricature of him?"

I feel the need to say something, even though I know I should just keep my mouth shut.

"He's a jerk and you know it," I add.

"He happens to be one of the most respected teachers at Saint Anselm's," Pablo says, "having taught generations of students to love and respect filmmaking. Including me."

Theo can't seem to leave this alone. "Okay, but he's also a cheater and a bully."

Pablo throws our script onto his desk. "That's it, Theo. One more comment and you and your partners won't be making any movie at all."

Priti stands up. "That's totally uncool, Pablo!"

Pablo is about to answer when the door opens. Mr. Beaverton is standing there.

"I am sorry to intrude, but all this shouting is very distracting to our class next door," he says in that annoyingly calm, deep voice.

Pablo smooths out his corduroy jacket. "We were having . . . creative differences."

Mr. Beaverton smiles, which is even creepier. "Well, try and control your class, Pablo. Really, now. It's only a student film, right, kids? Nothing to yell about."

He gives a little bow and closes the door behind him.

Priti has clearly made a decision. "The Beaver can go," she says.

Theo glares at her.

"Thank you, Priti. That's my last note," Pablo says quietly, with none of his usual lightness.

The bell rings, and we collect our things.

I turn to Priti. "I guess we had no choice."

"That's what I thought, but Theo is going to take some convincing," she says.

I don't need to turn around to know that he has disappeared as usual.

"The Beaver was truly the most unkindest cut of all," Priti says.

I nod, knowing that she won't be able to resist.

"Did you know that expression comes from Shakespeare?" she adds.

My moment of triumph has arrived at last. "Yes! I *do* know that, Priti! It's from Marc Antony's speech about Brutus stabbing Julius Caesar!"

Priti looks confused and impressed at the same time, if that's possible.

As we walk down the hallway to the stairs, I can't stand it. "We both learned it in Mr. Halverson's English class last year!"

"Wait. You were in my English class last year?" Priti asks.

There is a crash somewhere down the stairs.

Priti makes a face. "What was that?"

I want to say, "That was the last piece of my self-esteem being destroyed," but instead I just say, "Someone must have dropped a lunch tray."

CHAPTER 24

The Watcher

When you see people shooting a movie, like in a behind-the-scenes or "making of" video, you usually just concentrate on the director looking through the camera, or maybe the special-effects guys working all the puppets they will later replace with computer-generated monsters or superheroes or whatnot.

It's a whole lot different when *you're* the person shooting the film. There are all sorts of decisions that have to be made, and in our case, when we're all supposed to take on different roles for different scenes, it's a lot harder than it looks. We decide to just take turns being the director. I thought Theo would have balked at the idea of being in charge, but it turns out he likes telling other people what to do.

Persephone got Cammi to help us with the costumes, since he works in the costume shop and can pretty much make anything. Noel was a little bent out of shape because we're "on the other team," but Cammi is tight with Persephone, so he couldn't really say anything.

It's no fun being either the cameraman or the sound guy. Even though we're using digital cameras so we can see if we get it all right, it's still hard to make sure everything is in focus and framed properly.

And if you're the sound person, you have a pole with the microphone at the end of it, which you hold over the actors' heads, just out of sight of the camera's lens. It's hard work and your arms ache after standing there motionless, especially if you need more than one take to get it right.

We only have two days, and we're using a lot of high schoolers and teachers who don't have a lot of patience and are really busy. But everybody seems to think it's really funny and loves the way they look in their costumes.

The tea party in the faculty lounge is especially good, with all the teachers really getting into it. I don't know if Persephone has to act that much since they're acting so weird and bizarre (of course Mr. Bergstrom is always weird, so he's perfect as the Mad Hatter).

The other scenes go really well, and we are actually on schedule to finish by the end of the day, which is important because we have to give the equipment to Ralph and Noel and Cammi for their giant sword fight thing.

As Priti and I watch the playback of the scenes we've

already shot, we turn to each other and she gives me a thumbs-up. We haven't edited it or added music or anything, but already it's looking really good.

I hate to admit it, but all of Pablo's changes made it better. I mean, we all miss the Beaver, but at the same time it really doesn't hurt the story not having it in there.

Still, Theo can't resist wearing a T-shirt he's clearly had custom printed that says I MISS THE BEAVER.

Even Pablo laughs when he sees it.

We're down to the last shot, and we've saved it because we're going to be shooting outside. It's right at the beginning of the story, where Persephone sees the white rabbit, who's late for his class.

Priti has gotten Jensen to play the part, and he looks really awesome in his fancy velvet coat, vest, and rabbit ears, holding a giant watch.

All we need to get is Persephone walking down Montague Street, which is the main business area near Saint Anselm's, lined with restaurants, banks, and phone stores.

What that means is we're kind of drawing a crowd. There are kids from eighth grade, friends of Jensen, and businesspeople glancing over at us as they pass. Lexie is also here, as moral support.

We set up the camera. Theo is the director, and I'm the cameraman. Priti doesn't seem to mind holding the boom mic (as it's called) for Jensen and Persephone's scene. Persephone starts to walk into frame and the camera follows her up Montague Street. She turns and sees something.

Now we have to set up our next shot, which is Jensen. He's been busy talking with his friends, and Priti waves him over.

We move the camera, and Theo yells "Action!" just like a real movie director (by now we've stopped being self-conscious about saying it).

Jensen is muttering to himself and scratching his big rabbit ears. I can see out of the corner of my eye that Priti is doing her best not to laugh, but the boom mic moves into the shot, and we have to do it again. Priti swears she will get it right next time.

We do the shot again, and this time, Jensen catches Priti's eye and cracks up.

Lexie wanders over. "Listen, I can hold that pole thing if Priti isn't going to be able to get through this," she whispers.

I should point out that Lexie is not the best whisperer, and even over the traffic outside, Priti hears this and says, "No way! I am going to do this. I am *so* sorry."

It's completely unlike Priti to be the one to mess up, but I'm pretty sure it's because Jensen is here.

We do one more take, and Persephone is perfect as ever, turning to the camera and saying "Curiouser and curiouser!" And then following Jensen up the street toward Saint Anselm's.

As she goes up the street, getting smaller and smaller in the viewfinder, Theo yells "Cut!" and everyone applauds.

We play the scene back and it looks really good. Maybe a little out of focus in places, but that's okay because it's supposed to be a dream. At least that's what we tell Pablo, who nods. Theo takes the camera off the tripod and hands it carefully to Pablo.

"Don't worry, Theo," he says, "I'm locking it up in the school office. No one is touching the memory card until I upload it to the Web tonight."

Theo nods absentmindedly and Pablo puts everything in the camera bag, and since we're so close to the school, Pablo says he has no problem taking it back for us.

Normally I would expect Theo to say something about wanting to be there to make sure the office is locked securely, or insisting on taking the memory card home (something kids are forbidden to do—there have been years where three days of footage has disappeared when a memory card got lost or broken).

But Theo is totally not caring.

Pablo heads back to school, and I turn to Theo.

He is distracted by something.

Lexie is too.

"What's up?" I ask.

"That guy," Theo says. "The one in the purple polo shirt. He's been watching us this whole time. He hasn't taken his eyes off us."

I follow his eyes and see a middle-aged balding guy, the sun shining off his sweaty head. He has a gut, making his shirt resemble a giant grape. He notices us staring back at him and ducks into a nearby drugstore.

Theo chews his thumbnail. "Okay, I need to know who that is and why he was watching us."

"Yeah, that is totally weird. Why would he be staring at us?" I say.

I turn and see Lexie looking at Theo and me. "You guys are idiots."

She has an expression that I can't quite read. It's both sad and ticked off. "He wasn't staring at you."

"He was looking over here the whole time," Theo insists. "I kept checking."

Lexie shakes her head. "He was looking over here all right—he just wasn't looking at *you*."

Theo is getting impatient. "So if you know so much, what was he looking at?"

"He was looking at Priti," Lexie says simply, as if it was the most obvious thing in the world.

CHAPTER 25

I Get Schooled

Theo looks at Lexie like she has two heads. "That's ridiculous. Why would he be spending all that time looking at Priti?"

I look over at Priti and she's got her arms wrapped around her chest. Jensen has rushed over and is putting his coat over her bare shoulders. She looks like she's going to cry. I've never seen her look so vulnerable.

All of sudden it's so obvious that I feel like an idiot.

Jeez, the guy must have been at least forty. And he was ogling Priti this whole time.

"Wow," I say.

Theo is as dense as ever. "What *are* you guys talking about?"

"Theo, you are as dumb as a pile of bricks. He was staring at Priti because he was—how can I say this in terms you'll understand?" Lexie says. "He was . . . breaching her security."

Theo ponders this for a moment. "Ooohhh. I think I get it."

"Good," Lexie says.

With Jensen's coat wrapped around her shoulders, Priti heads back to the school. Lexie is helping me stuff props and bits of costume into a big trunk from the drama department.

"That's so disgusting," I say. "I mean, that guy . . ."

Lexie looks very tired. Her shoulders droop. "It's not just that guy. It happens *every day*. You just don't see it."

"Oh, please," I say. "Not *every* day."

Lexie drops Persephone's wig into the trunk. "Alex, do yourself a favor and shut up."

I can't let this drop. "But not at school, right?"

"Are you kidding me?" Lexie practically screams. "It happens at school like all the time! Gah! Open your eyes sometime, Alex Davis."

"Okay, but . . . ," I allow. "I mean, Priti's T-shirt is pretty tight. I can understand why—"

Lexie grabs the handle of the costume trunk and stomps off.

"What? What did I say?" I ask.

"I really thought you were a better person," she calls back. "You're just another *guy*."

Theo gives me a "you really messed this up" look and follows her.

Well, that kind of stung. "What the heck? I was just stating a fact," I say.

I hear a voice behind me. "No, you weren't. *Think*. Think about what you were saying."

I turn and see Mom holding Violet's hand. She must have wandered over here after the lower school let out.

Well, this is uncomfortable. "I was just saying I understand why someone would stare, that's all."

Mom sighs and looks toward the drugstore. "I heard the whole thing, Alex. Let me ask you something. Do you really think it's fair to blame Priti for that grown man's behavior? He's an adult. He should know better."

"I didn't say that!" I protest.

"You kind of did," Mom answers. "Can't you understand why Lexie is so mad?"

"Girls should get to wear whatever they want," Violet says, although I doubt she understands what we're talking about.

I'm about to say this when suddenly I realize I agree with her. But I'm still mad.

I don't know why, maybe because I'm ashamed of saying what I did, but I feel the urge to say something mean.

I think of Lexie in her ratty, oversized T-shirts. "I don't know why Lexie acts like such an expert. I mean, it's not like *she* ever gets stared at," I say.

I expect my mom to tell me to watch my mouth, like she usually would.

But instead she stops right there on the sidewalk and looks me in the eye. "What makes you think she doesn't?"

I am about to laugh when I look at some men who are passing Lexie up ahead of us. For the first time, I see—really *see*—the expressions on their faces as they look at Lexie up and down. It's so gross it makes me feel sick. Who are these men? Why is no one yelling at them?

"That is so awful," I say. "I never knew about this stuff."

My mom gives my arm a reassuring squeeze. A "we are okay but seriously you need to do better" squeeze.

Up ahead, I see Lexie is having trouble with the big costume trunk.

My mom nudges me. "Looks like she could use your help."

I nod and run up to Lexie, who is panting and struggling to carry what is clearly a two-person job. Theo has not volunteered to help.

"Hey," I say softly. "You were right. I am a jerk." I take hold of the other handle on the trunk.

"Sounds like your mom was giving you a little lesson," Lexie says, adding quickly, "Not that I was listening or anything."

We count to three and pick up the trunk. It is definitely heavier than I thought. "I can't take back what I said, but I can try to do better."

"Apology accepted," Lexie says simply. And I know she means it. That's the nice thing about knowing someone so well. She can't help adding, "Better late than never."

I want to get things back to normal. "So . . . speaking of never, you never seem to talk about Video Games class. How's it going?"

Lexie hangs her head. "Yeah. That. It seemed really cool at first, but Bridgeman is really . . . not a great teacher. It feels like he's just a few chapters ahead of us, learning stuff as he teaches it. We haven't gotten to make our own games yet. It's so boring. I swear, you probably know more than he does about gaming."

I try not to look too smug.

"Believe me, you are so lucky you didn't get it," Lexie says. "Filmmaking is so much more fun."

As always, Lexie is right. "Yeah, funny how that worked out."

We are interrupted by a large commotion at the front door. There is yelling from Felix's contingent. He is looking up from his phone and sharing something with the others.

As I approach, Felix looks up at me, a wild, triumphant expression on his face.

"I just got a text from my mom! She has a friend in Councilman Randolph's office and she says he's going to vote against the Court Street Towers!"

///////

By the time I come home, there's the sound of opera music blaring from my mom's home office and Violet is happily on the living room couch with her tablet.

Whenever my mom is up against a hard deadline with a greeting card project, this is the drill. Playing opera music means "I am working and do not come in and disturb me unless you are bleeding profusely and your father isn't home."

We tried to get her to wear headphones or earbuds, but she says they hurt her ears, so we put up with it.

Violet is thrilled because she can spend hours on the tablet making gardens in *Farm Maker* or whatever app she's devoted to this week.

I mean, at her age, shouldn't she be reading a book or something?

I made the mistake of suggesting this to Mom once, who then turned to Violet and said, "Look! Your big brother is volunteering to read to you while I'm in the office!"

After that, I learned to keep my mouth shut about Violet.

I head to my room and actually have most of my homework finished when I hear the front door open, meaning Dad is home.

I hear Violet squeal and the opera music turn off briefly.

Then I hear it resume and there's a soft knock on the door.

"Come in," I say.

A great thing about my parents is that they have a rule with me that started when I was twelve.

"We will never just walk into your room," my dad promised. "We will knock and wait for you to say 'come in.'"

"Unless you give us reason not to trust you, we will," my mom added.

I don't know why I'm so lucky. A lot of my friends have parents with like zero boundaries. Even Lexie's folks don't let her keep her door closed. Weird, right?

I asked why once and my mom started to tell me a story

about when my grandparents barged into my dad's room when he was twelve and it was really embarrassing, although they wouldn't say why, and when I asked why, my mom was laughing so hard my dad said, "Can we just drop this?"

I'm just glad they have kept their side of the bargain. And I try not to give them a reason to not trust me. The worst I do is sneak snacks into my room, which drives my mom nuts, but I said, "I could be doing drugs" (we had health class that day), and that kind of made her feel like snacks weren't all that bad on the scale of things.

My dad pops open the door and the smell of Chinese takeout wafts into my room.

"Hey! Dinner prep time," Dad announces.

I close my algebra book and jump off my bed. (There is no greater feeling than your parents coming into your room and finding you doing your homework instead of the game you would have been playing if they'd come in ten minutes later, which then would have meant a whole conversation about how much time you're wasting playing computer games.)

My job is to set the table, with all the bowls and chopsticks and stuff. I fold the paper napkins and make each place setting look like a real restaurant. We want it to look nice when Mom comes out of her office.

Dad has divided the food into different serving dishes, and we get to pick our own food (except for Violet, of course, who is given heaps of baby corn and an egg roll and some dumplings, which keeps her busy for most of the meal).

I wait until the right moment and then say, "Hey, Dad, Felix told me something about the Towers project."

"What's that?" he asks, paying half attention while he hunts for the baby corn in the mixed vegetables.

"His mom texted him that someone in Councilman Randolph's office said he's voting against the project."

There is a plop as the baby corn my dad speared falls off his fork. My dad is staring at me motionless.

"That's impossible. He hasn't even gotten a report from us yet. Dan hasn't made a determination yet. I know that for a fact. We haven't even had a preliminary vote."

Dad looks genuinely weirded out by this news.

"Maybe they heard wrong," I suggest.

"I hope so," my dad says. "But I would love to know who that 'friend in the office' was. Sounds like someone spreading false information."

I nod. "Yeah, totally."

I hear the phone ringing. We usually don't answer it during dinner since the only people to use that line are spammers or my grandparents, who are just like all grandparents and prefer to call the "real phone."

I hear my mom pick up in her office. She comes out holding the receiver to her ear, using her "I'm talking to a client or someone from your school" voice.

"I'm so glad to hear it! Alex just loves the class. He can't stop talking about it." She looks up. "He's right here. Hold on!"

Mom hands me the phone. "It's Pablo. For you."

Is there anything weirder than your teacher calling you at home?

I put it to my ear. "Hey! What's up?"

"Just checking with you, Alex. You didn't change the memory card before you handed me the camera, right?"

I laugh. "Jeez, Pablo, you only told us a hundred times to leave it in the camera. Why would I take it out anyway?"

There is a pause.

"So . . . you don't have it."

"Um . . . no . . . ," I say, dreading where this is going.

"Okay, we have a problem," Pablo says. "There is no data on the memory card in your camera."

CHAPTER 26

Call the Doctor

We agree to meet at school the next day before class.

I arrive in time to hear Pablo grilling Priti. "Are you *sure* no one else touched the camera before Theo gave it to me?"

"I wasn't paying attention," Priti admits. "I was doing sound, remember?"

I interrupt, speaking to Pablo. "You made a big deal of promising Theo no one would touch it and you were locking it in the closet yourself."

Pablo is holding the camera we used. He shows the screen on the back.

When he presses the PLAY button, a message pops up on a dark screen: *No valid images on card.*

"Could it be a problem with the camera?" I ask.

Pablo looks grim. He pops the card out of the camera and puts it into one of the computers we're going to use to edit our films. The same message appears.

"But you saw—" Priti says.

She turns away and is clearly trying to figure this out.

She turns back. "Are you sure *you* didn't erase the data by mistake?"

"Priti, I've been doing this a long time. I mean, everyone makes mistakes, but that's why at the end of the shoot, we always lock the card."

Pablo is right. There is a little switch on the side of the card that you flip up to lock the card so it can't be used to record on anymore.

I look around. "Where's Theo anyway?"

"I left a voice mail for him. As a matter of fact, a few. I guess he had more important things to do," Pablo says in a tight voice. I think he's a little tired of Theo's attitude.

Priti is flipping through her book. "There's only one thing to do. Reshoot. I can start calling people and setting that up."

"I'm afraid that's impossible," Pablo says. "The cameras are all reserved for other students' projects."

Priti whirls around. This is a girl who is not used to people saying no to her. "Then we'll buy a new camera."

"I can't let you do that," Pablo says. "It wouldn't be fair to the others."

I pick up the camera. "Not fair? It's not our fault the data is gone."

"Who's using this one?" Priti asks.

Pablo checks the sign-up sheet. "Noel and RPG."

"But RPG's family has professional cameras. They can lend him one," Priti says.

Pablo is about to answer when he catches Priti's look of determination. "I . . . I'll talk to Mr. Beaverton and see if we can bend the rules."

"Oh, *great*," I say. "He definitely strikes me as the type to bend the rules, especially for one of *your* students."

Theo wanders into the room, whistling. He seems totally unfazed.

"Dude, did you not get the message about the memory card?" I ask.

He drops his laptop case on the desk next to mine and takes a seat. "Huh? Oh . . . yeah. That's really a bummer."

Priti stands over him, hands on hips. "You're not the least bit concerned about this? We just lost all the footage from our film! Erased! *Gone!*"

Theo ignores her and takes out his laptop.

Priti looks like she's going to shake him like Alice shook the Red Queen.

Theo looks over at Pablo. "One question. No one's used that card since it was erased, right?"

Pablo nods.

Theo leans back and takes us in. "Listen, guys, here's the thing. When a memory card's data is erased, like if someone deliberately deleted the data on our card—I'm not saying they did, just supposing—as long as no one has used the card, the data is still there. It just has to be recovered."

Pablo glares at Theo. "Theo. Please. Don't you think I tried using our data-recovery software? There's nothing there to recover."

"We'll see," Theo says, and snaps his fingers. "Can I have the card?"

Before Pablo can explode, Theo adds, "Please?"

Pablo pops the card out of his computer and hands it to Theo.

Theo leans down and inserts it into a slot in his laptop. There is a whirring sound.

A screen pops up with a stethoscope and the words *Recovery Doctor.*

All sorts of warnings and sign-in screens whirl by as Theo types in passwords at lightning speed. "This isn't a job for consumer-grade recovery software," Theo says. "This is top-shelf stuff. Super proprietary."

Priti's eyes narrow. "If it's so special, how did you get it?"

"That's my little secret," Theo says. "Anyhow, it doesn't matter. I tweaked it and improved the algorithm."

We gather around the screen and watch as the program he's opened comes to life.

A message pops up that says *Scanning disk . . .*

It turns to green and now reads *500 GB of data found. Recover: Y/N?*

Theo turns to Pablo with a smirk. "I assume I should press *Y*?"

Pablo nods, and Theo does. After a few minutes, the screen changes to *Data recovered. Do you wish to view it?*

Theo closes the program and ejects the card. It pops out and he hands it to Pablo. "There you go."

Pablo looks at the card and then puts it in the computer. Our footage shows up, safe and sound. Priti lets out a soft "whooo" and falls back in her chair.

"You're welcome," Theo says.

Priti gazes at Theo like a kid who's seen their first magic trick. "That was amazing!"

The bell rings and the other kids are gathered in the hall, staring through the glass in the door.

I go to let them in, and Pablo stops me.

"Just a second," he says, sounding deadly serious. "Okay, Theo, how do you want to do this?"

Theo looks baffled. "Do what?" He is packing up his laptop.

"Do we go down to the middle school office and I have one of the security guards search you? Or are you going to give it to me?"

Theo laughs nervously. "Give you what? Um, lighten up, Pablo. I'm so sorry I flexed on you like that. But next time—"

"Give me the card," Pablo says flatly. He holds out his hand.

"What card?" Theo says.

Someone raps on the door. Without turning around, Pablo calls out, "Just a minute!" He turns back to Theo. "The bell to start class is going to ring in two minutes. That's all the time and patience I have left. Now, do you want to stay at Saint Anselm's or not?"

I have no idea what's going on, but clearly it's *not good*.

Priti has figured it out, though. Of course.

"Give him the other memory card," she tells Theo.

Theo looks at her. He reaches into his pocket and pulls out a memory card and throws it on Pablo's desk. "I was going to tell you."

"You need to be more careful, Theo," Pablo says. "Did you think I wouldn't notice that you handed me a SanDisk Extreme PLUS?"

I look at the card on the table, the one that had no data on it. Its label reads *SanDisk Extreme PLUS*.

"You had the original card from the camera in your laptop the whole time," I say. "You just pretended to switch them out."

Theo nods. "Bingo."

"So when did you switch the cards in the camera?" Pablo asks.

"He did it when he took the camera off the tripod," Priti says. "We were all so busy packing up. He just popped it out and replaced it."

"But why?" I demand. "What was the point?"

Theo snaps forward in his chair. His eyes are glued on Pablo. "Opsec. Remember what I told you? I was assessing the project's vulnerabilities. Once I determined that the current level of security was insufficient, I knew the only way that card would be safe was if I had it. And I had to demonstrate to Pablo its weaknesses."

Pablo strides over to the metal door of the locker. "What

weaknesses? The cameras are all in here. Locked up in this closet all night. They're secure."

"Like that's supposed to make me feel better?" Theo laughs.

He joins Pablo at the closet and pulls two small thin pieces of metal from his pocket. He inserts one into the lock and holds it tightly, while pushing the longer pick into the lock and raking it back and forth. In a matter of seconds, he's turned the handle and the closet door is open.

"That's kid stuff," Theo says.

The door opens and the other kids stream in as Theo returns to his desk while Pablo stares after him, speechless.

CHAPTER 27

The Daring Exploits of the Jolly Roger

Of course, by the time the class is over, Theo's little stunt is known by pretty much everyone in the seventh grade. Nathan and Mateo beg him to teach them how to pick locks ("Watch YouTube," Noel tells them, insisting that *he* could have picked that lock if he wanted to). Mr. Beaverton hears about it and insists on a meeting with the head of school. Considering the head of school is in our movie (we even got her to say "Off with their heads!" which is going to be a guaranteed laugh, I *bet* you), I don't think Theo is too concerned.

But of course the majority of kids had the exact same reaction: "There's a kid named Theo in our class?"

And *I* was mad Priti didn't remember me from English!

The bottom line is that we got our footage back and

uploaded it to the school server. This means I can start working on our rough cut. The rough cut is where you just put all the scenes in the right order, without worrying about things like music or sound effects or fancy credits or even fade-ins and fade-outs. It's just to see how the story works.

I know it won't take long.

Since I already have the editing software at home, Pablo gave me special permission to work on it after school instead of having to sign out a computer.

After dinner, I sit down to download the files I need for the scene I'm going to edit.

I hear a *bing* and notice that Theo's sent a text.

I check it.

Use this link to sign in. More secure.

I copy and paste the link and get to the Saint Anselm's site. It asks me to sign in online with the new password. Theo has changed the password for our project pretty much every day, because he feels it's more "secure" that way.

I do and type in the address for the server.

The last scene we shot is downloaded first.

It's going to take a while to download all the footage I need (these files are *big*!), so I get to work looking at the raw footage as the rest of the files load in.

I watch the takes where the mic is in the shot, where someone giggles, and then I get to the good take. This one is really good. But I watch it again. Argh.

There are some figures moving around in the background. It's a little distracting. Why didn't I see that when we were shooting the scene? I might be able to fix it by zooming in on the frame.

That's going to take some work, so I head to the kitchen to get a snack first.

My dad is at the kitchen table going over some plans from one of the projects he's helping to evaluate. In the bathroom, I hear Violet screaming with laughter. No doubt she's just doused Mom with water from the plastic cup they use to rinse her hair. If I had done that when I was her age, I would have been in so much trouble, but I hear Mom saying, "Oh, thank you! I needed to wash my hair tonight! You just saved me so much time!"

She gets away with murder, I tell you.

Just as I'm thinking this, I notice Dad is no longer looking at his plans. I guess I wasn't paying attention when his phone rang.

He's looking really serious. He says "Hold on" to whoever he's talking to and turns to me. "You're not downloading anything from the Internet, are you?"

"Yeah, from the school server," I tell him. "Why?"

Dad runs into my room and I follow him. He's at my keyboard, asking the person on the other end of the phone what to do. "Yes. Okay. I've done that."

I watch as he shuts down my browser.

"Hey!" I say. "I need those files."

Dad acts like I'm not even in the room. "Yes. All right. Let me go to the Wi-Fi router."

I trail after him as he strides into Mom's office, where the router lives. He pulls the power cord out of the back. "That's it. Yes, it's unplugged. All right. Let me know."

He clicks off the phone and puts it on the table and stares at it like it's a rattlesnake or something.

"What the heck is going on?" I demand.

"That was Roger," Dad says, still looking at the phone like it's possessed by demons.

I met Roger once. He was introduced as "the guy who keeps the computers running." My dad told me his nickname at the office was the Jolly Roger because no one ever saw him crack a smile. "The IT guy from the office?"

My dad finally manages to tear his eyes away from the phone. "He's not just IT. He's actually our infosec guy."

He sees my confused look. "Infosec. Information security. It's Roger's job to make sure all the computers attached to our servers at work are secure. He says there's been an exploit."

"That sounds exciting!" I say. Dad loves a good joke.

Usually.

Not tonight.

"Alex, this is really, really bad. It means someone's hacked into our router. Somehow they were able to bypass our security."

"How?" I ask.

"That's what he's trying to figure out. He traced it to our router from the office. Someone was trying to access our files, and luckily he was able to stop the attack before they installed any malicious software or removed or changed anything."

"Why?" I ask.

"There are millions of dollars at stake with a lot of the projects that we oversee. These developers borrow money from banks on the understanding that we're going to let them build," Dad explains. "That's why Roger is so important. And the investors in these projects aren't just American. There is money flowing in from all over."

"Like from where?" I ask.

We've moved back into the living room. He picks up some papers. "This one has money from Russia. This one from France. This one from China."

Mom walks in with Violet, wrapped in a towel and clutching her tablet, howling.

"Honey, is the Internet out?" Mom asks over the noise.

"Read her a book, please!" my dad calls back. "I'll tell you about it later."

"But Daddy does the voices better!" Violet whines.

"I'll be upstairs in a little while," Dad says, kissing her. "I need to do something with Alex right now."

"Don't take too long," my mom pleads as she drags Violet off to her room.

Dad's phone vibrates on the table. He jumps like it bit him.

I can't help it. He looks so funny, I smile.

"Wipe that smile off your face, mister. This is serious," my dad says.

He checks the number on the phone and answers it. "Yes, Roger. Okay. Uh-huh. Yes, I'll ask him. No problem. Glad to hear it."

He puts down the phone and takes a deep breath. "Okay, Alex. It seems like nothing was breached. But if Roger hadn't been there working late, they would have had access to all our confidential data and files all night."

Now it's my turn to take a deep breath. "Okay, that's scary. But how?"

My dad walks me into my room and sits on my bed. "Okay, walk me through what happened."

I tell him about logging onto the Saint Anselm's server.

"Anything different?"

"Dad, I told you about Theo. He's kind of a nut about security himself. He texted me right before I went on and sent me a new link . . ."

My voice trails off.

My dad reaches over to my desk and takes my phone. He carefully copies and pastes the link and turns to me.

"Send that to me in an email, please."

I do as he says, and he takes his phone and quickly types something.

His phone rings and he answers. "Yes, Roger? I thought so."

Dad turns to me. "That link takes you to a spoof page."

I look at my screen. "A what page?"

"A spoof page. It's set up to look exactly like a real page. Usually Amazon or Netflix or some big company. They tell you your identity has been compromised and get you to type in your password info and then they're in."

"Oh, you mean phishing," I say. "I know all about that.

They try and do it all the time with me. I just delete those emails. They're so obvious."

My dad leans back onto my pillow. "Well, they got you this time."

"You mean someone set up a fake Saint Anselm's page just to get my passwords and stuff?" I ask.

"Once you signed into that screen, they had a back door into our whole home network," Dad says.

"How do you know so much about this?" I ask.

"Roger gave us all a seminar on Internet security a few months ago. I just never thought it would really happen, you know?"

I think for a second. "But . . . does that mean Theo set me up? He's the one who sent the text."

"It's not that simple. You can spoof a text as well," Dad tells me. "They can send a text that looks like it's coming from your cell phone provider, so why not from your friend?"

I was going to say "Theo isn't my friend" but realized that was a little off topic right now.

"Call him," Dad says. "See if he sent the text."

"Um . . . he doesn't have it set up to accept voice calls, just text," I explain.

My dad gets up and walks back into the living room. "This kid sure is obsessed with security."

I watch as he goes to where we keep the school directory.

"What are you doing, Dad?" I ask.

He is thumbing through the pages. "I'm going to call his parents. Maybe we can talk to him that way."

"Good luck with that," I say as he looks down at the names.

"No phone number. That's weird," my dad muses.

"Yeah, and his dad seems to work for an infosec company," I say. "You think?"

My dad stares at the page. "Honestly, Alex, I don't know what to think."

CHAPTER 28

The Most Unkindest Rough Cut of All

Theo stares at the text on my phone. "I cannot believe you fell for this."

"Like it's *my* fault?" I say, grabbing my phone back. "If you weren't so impossible to reach—"

Lexie and I were walking to school when we spotted Theo sitting by the window of a nearby coffee place, laptop in front of him. As soon as we approached, he closed the lid.

"So you're *sure* no one used your phone?" Lexie asks.

Theo looks at her like she's an idiot. "What do *you* think?"

"Look, someone sent me that message, and it ended up shutting down the entire building commissioner's office for like three hours until the infosec guy cleared the network."

I see Theo's mouth twitch when I say the word *infosec*. "So this . . . infosec guy. How good is he? I mean, is he just an IT guy who pokes around or—"

I decide to bluff. "No, he's the real deal."

Theo visibly relaxes. "That's good. Very good. Whoever did this, they aren't amateurs."

"Can you trace it back to the original spoofer?" Lexie asks.

Theo thinks for a second. "I'll work on that, but it's going to be really hard. Especially if they're using masking software and most likely an untraceable ISP."

I glance at my phone and see that we have maybe ten minutes before first period.

"We need to get to school," I say. "But we can continue this in film class."

Theo licks his lips. "Uh . . . you guys go on ahead. I have a free first period. Got something to do."

Lexie and I walk in the direction of school. Suddenly, Lexie does a quick U-turn and runs back to the table Theo is sitting at. As she approaches, he slams down the screen on his laptop again. He stands up and Lexie backs off, hands in front of her.

She comes back to me, grinning. "Boy, was he not happy to see me again! I told him you thought you left your phone there. I don't think he believed me."

"So did you see anything?" I ask.

Lexie thinks for a second. "There was this message on his screen I caught right before he closed it, saying 'I hacked Alex's father's network.' You think that's a *clue*?"

Lexie, as usual, cracks herself up.

As we reach the front door of the school, Priti breaks off from Jensen and her real friends and comes to join us. "How did it go last night?"

I catch her up on all the drama.

"Wow. So you really think Theo had something to do with that?" Priti asks.

Lexie looks at her and nods. "I'm starting to wonder about him."

"The important thing is that we have the footage," Priti says.

We head upstairs. "But now I have to do all the editing here at school."

"Stinks to be you," Lexie says helpfully as she and Priti wander off to their respective first periods.

/////

Pablo still hasn't quite recovered from the memory card incident with Theo. He's been really sharp with him, so I try to be the peacemaker. Today, as usual, Theo is nowhere to be seen.

"Look, Pablo, I know what Theo did was bad, but I think he's got issues," I say.

There is a crash from the corner where Joie and Oona have been practicing backflips.

Pablo turns back to me. "That's too bad, because I have an issue with him."

"He's very paranoid, and I think it was his way of proving how insecure Saint Anselm's is."

"That's no excuse for putting all of us through what he did," Pablo said. "Besides, who would want to erase your data?"

"I can think of a few people," Priti says, taking her usual seat. "Considering how many people want to win this. Or want one of their students to win it."

Pablo closes the door. "Be careful of making baseless accusations, Priti. I'm surprised. It's not like you."

"All I'm saying is that you yourself said how our film could win the Golden Reel this year," Priti says. "I'm just going on what you said."

Pablo clasps his hands behind his back. "Well, it's not going to win anything until it's edited." He calls out to the various teams. "All right! Time to get to your workstations!"

We head over to our assigned computer and call up the files from the network. Yes, just as the bell rings, Theo has mysteriously appeared.

We begin going through the various takes and selecting which ones are the best.

I can't help thinking this would be so much faster at home, but it's still nice to feel Priti looking over my shoulder. I can't tell if it's her shampoo or if she's wearing perfume, but she smells really nice.

There is no way on this earth that I would ever tell her that. I'm just saying it here because it's true.

The forty-five minutes speed by and we've practically got an entire rough cut finished.

The other teams have barely gotten through two scenes.

Nathan and Mateo are too busy laughing at their own work.

Oona and Joie and Jojo are arguing about whether or not to show every vault in slow motion.

And RPG and Noel and Cammi are stuck on putting in their special effects, even though this is supposed to be a rough cut.

Meanwhile, I'm putting the finishing touches on the final scene. I notice, again, something distracting in the background that I still can't make out.

Priti is shaking her head. "You are so good at this. You'll have to teach me how to do it sometime."

I feel a rush as my cheeks turn red. Not that I'm all into Priti or anything anymore. That ship has sailed. But still . . . "S-sure. N-no problem. A-anytime. Just say wh-when," I stammer, somehow not knowing when to shut up.

Theo looks over from his phone. "Yeah, it's coming along."

Pablo wanders over from where he has been helping Nathan and Mateo cut their first scene. "You're already on the wake-up scene? Really?"

"I told you I was fast," I say, trying not to sound like a braggy little snot.

Okay, I fail.

I press SAVE and send it up to the cloud.

Theo leans in and types a few strokes on the keyboard. "You didn't save it in the right format."

I swat his hand away. "Theo, easy. I know what I'm doing. I've done like dozens of videos at camp. We want it saved in raw format until we've laid in the music and transitions and stuff. Then we compress it."

"I could have sworn it was the wrong codec," Theo says as the file loads in.

Halfway through, the file freezes.

We watch as a message pops up on the screen. *Transfer incomplete. File corrupted. Data lost.*

"What? Again?" Priti turns to Theo. "What did you do?"

"Me?" Theo says. "I didn't do anything!"

Priti is not going to be denied. "I saw you type something."

Theo shoves me out of the chair. I practically fall on the floor. "Ow!" I protest. "You could say *please.*"

"Shut up and let me do this," Theo mutters. His fingers are flying over the keyboard. I mean, I'm fast, but he's amazing. Files appear and disappear on the screen.

Priti and I watch mesmerized as Theo systematically goes through each individual clip we used to make the rough cut. He is running them through some sort of program he's called up.

Numbers scroll by, Y/N screens are answered, command lines appear and disappear.

Finally, Theo turns to us.

On the screen is the scene of Persephone and Jensen. The one I was working on.

"There's our culprit," Theo says. "Someone attached a virus to that file."

Theo presses a few more keys and a screen of commands pops up.

He peers at the code. "It's weird. It's only triggered when you press the save command."

"So is it something you can fix?" Priti asks.

"Yeah, give me a sec," Theo answers, calling up yet another sketchy-looking program.

This one has the picture of a showerhead and is called CodeCleaner.

Theo plugs the file into it.

There is a little scrubbing sound file and a *plink*.

Then a screen that says *File cleaned of malicious spyware* pops up.

"Spyware? Someone was spying on us?" I ask.

Theo quickly closes the program. "Nah. That's just what it says when it cleans up any malicious code. It was designed for corporate use, but I use it for everything."

Theo turns and motions us to lean in.

"I'm going to try something. Just go along with it," he whispers.

Priti knows better. "Theo, I don't trust you at all."

"Look, we want to catch whoever did this, right?" Theo asks. "This might be the only way."

Priti looks at me, and I shrug. "What's your plan?"

Instead of answering, like a normal kid might do, Theo yells a curse word really loudly, which has the desired effect of having Pablo run over to see what the problem is.

"I can't believe it," Theo howls.

Pablo peers at the screen. "What's wrong now, Theo?"

"The whole movie is ruined. All the files are corrupted for

some reason!" Theo says, mostly convincingly. I mean, convincingly enough that a grown-up might believe he was upset.

"All that work!" Priti wails, picking up her cue. "This means we'll never get to show our movie!"

The other kids from the class are slowly gathering around us.

Obviously I have to say something. "It was so good! We worked so hard on it."

I am *very* proud of the fact that I got my voice to break at the end of the last sentence.

Pablo is sitting at the computer. "Guys, just calm down. Everybody, go back to your work. I'll figure this out."

"Ha!" Theo snorts. "I'm telling you, those files are gone for real this time."

Pablo is in our folder, trying one file after another. I don't know how Theo did it, but once again all our files are inaccessible.

"This has never happened before," Pablo says, "but we'll get to the bottom of this, don't worry."

Theo turns to us, his long black hair hanging in his face, hiding his smile. "I sure hope so."

CHAPTER 29

Munchausen by What Now?

It's kind of touching how nice everyone is when they hear about what's happened to our files. Well, maybe *nice* isn't the right word to describe Persephone's reaction. *"My performance! Lost?"* she says. Dropping her tray so the whole lunchroom turns around.

Now she's got an audience.

"It can't be," she murmurs. "Tell me you're joking."

A tear wells up in her right eye. "I need air. I am suffocating!"

There is dead silence in the room. As we all have known Persephone for years, we've learned that you kind of have to let her have her moment.

Finally, it comes: "Noooooo!" she wails. "This can't be happening!"

"Jeez," Lexie grumbles. "Nobody died. Ease up already."

"Something precious *did* die, Alexandra," Persephone exclaims. "My work . . . my baby . . ."

"It was *our* film," I remind her.

Persephone turns to me. "Yeah, but my name was in the title."

Suddenly she gets an idea. "We can reshoot! Yes! My baby reborn!"

"There's no way we can get all the teachers and seniors together again," Priti says, "especially because it looks like it was something we did, since no one else's files were affected."

Persephone stops for a moment. Then a gleaming smile breaks across her face. "I know! I'll play all the parts! I can do it! Cammi can help with the costumes!"

"Um . . . I'm not sure we have the ability to pull that off," I say. "I mean, *you* could, of course. I'm talking about the technical stuff."

Persephone nods. "I see . . ."

Thankfully the rest of the lunchroom has lost interest once they've realized Persephone is not going to melt down.

Persephone goes to join her theater friends. Then she turns back. "Just think about it. I can do this, you know."

"Absolutely!" Priti says, and Persephone glows.

We watch her sweep off.

"She would too," Lexie says, dipping a chicken nugget (excuse me, this is Saint Anselm's. The menu calls them "select cuts of white meat chicken breaded and served with a variety of sauces," but they're not fooling anybody).

"Everything is working perfectly," Theo says, popping up out of nowhere.

Priti picks at her salad. It's something she's brought from home and looks like a thousand times better than what we're eating. "Okay, so what's the plan exactly?"

Theo eyes Lexie suspiciously. "How come she gets to stay?"

"First off, she knows all about what's going on," I say.

"You *told* her?" Theo practically jumps down my throat.

Priti dabs her mouth with a napkin. "No, I did."

"Do you really think I'd tell anyone?" Lexie says, shoving the nugget into her mouth and chewing loudly.

Theo gives her his trademark smirk. "You probably don't even understand how this all works."

Lexie swallows and wipes her mouth with her T-shirt (I notice Priti winces but doesn't say anything). "Oh yeah, Mr. Superspy? So, was it a direct action virus? Or a resident virus? The way Priti described it, it sounds like an overwrite virus."

Theo opens his mouth a few times like he's trying to decide how to answer this. Finally all he can say is: "How do you know all that stuff?"

Lexie looks at Priti. "When she told me what happened, I went online and looked up different types of computer viruses. It's pretty interesting."

Theo looks at me.

"She likes to learn stuff too," I say simply.

Before Theo can continue, Felix stops by the table on the way to bussing his tray.

"I heard what happened," he says. "It's heartbreaking."

This is very un-Felix-like. Priti smiles at him. "Thank you, Felix."

"I mean, not heartbreaking like people being kicked out of their homes by greedy developers . . . I mean, that's *really* heartbreaking, don't you agree?"

This, on the other hand, is very Felix. "You were at the meeting," I say. "Mr. Tolliver made a point over and over again to say that no one was being relocated or evicted."

Felix's eyes narrow. "Sure he says that. But I heard different. He's just like Hugh Hewitt. They're all the same."

Lexie can't resist. "Good thing it only affected these guys' film, huh? Yours is fine, I guess."

Felix nods. "Yep. I mean, if that virus had ruined *our* film, it would have been a *real* tragedy."

With that, he takes his tray and strides off.

Lexie looks after him. "What a jerk. So it *wasn't* a tragedy because it was your film?"

"I think he knows our film is his biggest competition," Priti says.

Theo nods. "And *I* think he'd do just about anything to make sure it isn't seen."

I cannot believe this. "You honestly think Felix would sabotage our film to win a stupid competition?"

"He was also furious that Persephone did our film instead of his, remember?" Priti says.

"And if he did win, it would give him a big platform for his political ideas," Lexie adds.

"All of this is just guessing. You have absolutely no evidence," I counter. "Besides, do any of us think he has the skills and knowledge to plant a sophisticated virus on a network like that?"

Everyone at the table considers what I said.

"No . . . but Noel does," Theo says. "And he seems like the kind of kid who might do it just to see if he could get away with it."

Lexie leans into the table. "Maybe they were working together!"

Priti frowns. "You think?"

"And maybe the Russians were in on it too!" I say. "This is so ridiculous. Nobody wants to win that badly."

"Beaverton does," Priti says. "Don't you think?"

Theo pops open his gross lunch and takes a swig. "As much as I'd love to pin this on that old fascist, I just don't think he has the ability. Not to do something like this. He's so old school."

"Well, *somebody* did it," I say. "And they're going to get a big surprise when we show up at the festival with our completed film."

Priti looks nervous. "So . . . when are we planning to tell Pablo?"

Theo drains his bottle. "Not until the very last moment. I don't trust him."

"You don't trust anybody, do you?" Lexie asks.

"Nope. That's why I made the files local only," Theo says.

I practically spit out my drink. "What? But that means we can't access the files online."

"That's right," Theo says. "And neither can anyone else. I'm taking no chances."

"So how do you plan on us working on the film?" Priti asks.

"Oh, that's easy," Theo replies. "We're going to break into the school tonight and put the files on a flash drive."

"Are you crazy?" I say loudly enough that kids from the other table turn around.

I look at Theo's drink. "Drinking that stuff for lunch? Every day? You're out of your mind."

The kids turn back to their food.

Theo doesn't answer. He looks around the lunchroom. "So we'll meet at the side entrance to the school at . . . let's say nine tonight."

"But it's locked," Priti says. Then she remembers who she's talking to. "This is so bad. I mean, if we get caught, we could be suspended."

"I've already scoped out the situation, and it will be fine."

"You've already broken into the school?" I ask.

"Not yet. I need your help for that. I wish it was a one-person job."

Priti shakes her head. "Nope. Nothing illegal. I won't do it."

"It's not *exactly* illegal," Theo says. "We're not stealing anything, just taking back our own property."

Lexie and Priti exchange looks.

Lexie stares down at the ground. "It's breaking and entering, Theo."

"I wouldn't risk you guys getting in trouble. I promise you it's safe," Theo says. "Trust me."

Before we can respond, he gets up and vanishes into the stream of kids leaving the room.

I'm trying to decide if Theo asking *us* to trust *him* is more ironic or moronic as I get up to drop off my tray.

Lexie motions me to sit down. She and Priti have locked eyes.

"Alex, there's one suspect we haven't talked about," Priti says.

I can't believe them. "Hey, I just know that one editing program! You don't really think I'd—"

"Not you, you dim bulb," Lexie says.

Then it hits me. Theo. "Ohhhhh . . . seriously? But why would he?"

Priti turns to me. "Alex, who else knows enough about viruses and computer security? He knows more than the teachers in the computer department, I bet. And you thought he might've broken into your network. If he's capable of that, why not this?"

"Sure, Theo *could* do it, but why the heck would he?" I ask.

Lexie and Priti answer at the exact same time. "Munchausen syndrome by proxy."

"Umm . . . what?" I ask, although I am vaguely aware of some of those words.

"I mean, not *literally*," Priti says.

"Totally," Lexie agrees. "The real thing is horrible! MSBP is where a parent deliberately makes their child sick in order to get attention and look like a caring, grieving parent."

"And if you think of our film like a child," Priti says, "maybe Theo is the one putting it in danger."

"So *he* can look like the hero?" I ask.

Priti and Lexie nod in unison, and when they do, a thought hits me. The two of them remind me of Violet's favorite dolls.

Priti is like her Bridal Barbie, the one she keeps in the cabinet and doesn't play with because she's too afraid to mess it up. Lexie is like her Elsa doll, the one she takes with her everywhere, who's a little messy from all the trips to the playground and all the dinners they've "shared." The Elsa doll might not be as glamorous and pristine, but it's clear which one is more important to Violet. Which one she really loves.

I'm turning all this over in my mind when Lexie waves her hand in front of my face.

"Hello? What are you thinking?" Lexie asks.

"Oh nothing," I lie.

I may be a dim bulb, but I'm not *that* dim.

CHAPTER 30

No One Will Ever Know

It's a lot harder than you think to explain to your parents why you have to be at school at nine p.m. I read in books all the time that kids sneak out of the house and have all sorts of adventures.

Try that when your parents stay up late to watch a movie or finish up some work they didn't get to that day.

Not so easy.

So Lexie and I just tell a little white lie and say we're working on the movie at Priti's house. We stay out after school and grab a slice of pizza for dinner.

It's been dark for hours by the time nine o'clock rolls around. There are deep shadows cast by the buildings surrounding our school. I never notice this stuff during the day, but at night it kind of gives me the creeps. Being a school night, Brooklyn Heights is pretty quiet now.

I would never tell her, but I'm glad Lexie is tagging along. I mean, I wouldn't want to wait here all by myself.

Theo warned us that he spotted a security camera shooting the door. We're to meet on the side of the building that doesn't have an entrance or a window. It's completely shrouded in darkness.

Lexie and I have just positioned ourselves against the wall when we see a figure dashing toward us. It ducks behind a car, and then when the light turns, it comes right at us.

Priti is dressed all in black, but it looks cool, not suspicious. Her face is flushed and she's out of breath. It's clear she's run all the way from her house, which is pretty close, but you do have to cross that six-lane monster that is Boerum Place.

Lexie reaches into her bag and hands Priti a bottle of water. Priti smiles at her gratefully and takes a sip. I watch her drink it and marvel that even all sweaty she looks perfectly groomed.

I also wish I'd thought of bringing water. Lexie thinks of everything.

"What did you tell your parents?" I ask Priti.

She turns and gives me one of her amazing smiles. "They are out for the evening at a big charity gala and won't be home until after midnight."

"What's the charity?" I ask.

Priti shrugs. "No idea. They go to so many."

"No babysitter?" Lexie asks.

"It's my Nani," Priti answers. "My dad's mom. She falls asleep in front of CNN every night. I left the light on in my room so even if she wakes up, she'll think I'm studying."

We stand there, looking into the thick glass of the entrance. Beyond us is a keypad with a flashing red light.

"I'm no security expert, but even if you get past the security camera, isn't that thing going to go off as soon as Superspy picks the lock?" Lexie says.

From the darkness, Special Agent Theo answers: "Yeah, usually it would."

He steps into the light with a backpack over his shoulder. He drops to the ground and looks up. "First things first."

Theo fishes around in his bag and pulls out something that looks like an industrial-size laser pointer.

He turns to Lexie. "You ever used one of these?"

Lexie takes it from him. "A laser pointer? Sure, to tease our cat. But—"

"This one is a lot more powerful," Theo tells her. "Alex tells me you totally own him at video games."

Lexie looks at me, amazed. "You told him *that*? I cannot believe you actually admitted that I'm better than you."

"Lexie, focus," I say, not wanting to give her the satisfaction.

Theo points a gloved hand at the security camera. "You see that lens?"

Lexie nods.

"You need to aim precisely at the center. It shouldn't be more than thirty seconds or so. But you need to keep holding it there. It will disable the camera just long enough for us to get in without being recorded. Can you do that?"

Lexie snorts. "Are you kidding? I beat the Water Temple in *Ocarina of Time* on the first try."

Theo shoots me a look. "Is that good?"

"It's the hardest level of all the *Legend of Zelda* games," I explain. "I was there or I wouldn't have believed it."

Priti nods. "I remember my brother playing it. It took him like two days to beat it."

"Just keep it aimed there until we're inside, okay?" Theo says.

Lexie salutes. "You bet."

"But what about the keypad in there?" I ask.

"Okay, so here's the thing," Theo says, pulling his laptop out of his bag and plugging a USB cable into it. He plugs a small white box into that. A green light glows on the box. "If we just open the door, it will trigger an alarm that will send a radio signal to the monitoring company, which contacts the police . . ."

Priti has it all figured out. "So if it's a radio signal, it can be jammed?"

Theo looks at her admiringly and nods.

The fact that she's wearing a skintight black catsuit doesn't register with him, but *this* he admires.

Theo points to the little plastic thingy hanging from his laptop. "This gizmo sends radio noise, which prevents the signal from getting through from the sensors to the control panel and tripping the alarm."

He turns to me. "As soon as I pick the lock, you press this button on the side of the box and then I'll open the door."

I nod. Priti cradles the laptop in her arms. I put my hand on the little plastic box.

I hope Priti doesn't notice how sweaty my hands are.

We're standing close enough that I can see her chest rising and falling. I look up and she gives me a nervous smile.

"Well, we're in it now, I guess."

Theo has taken his lock-picking tools from his bag and turns to us. "All right. Everyone ready?"

We each nod.

Theo takes a deep breath. "Three . . . two . . . one . . . *go!*"

Lexie aims the laser pointer at the camera and Theo dashes over to the door. He fiddles with the top lock and within seconds it turns.

He then turns to the lower lock, which is giving him a little more trouble. He tries another tool.

I look over and see that Lexie is biting her lip, trying to keep the laser steady.

Theo stops and grabs the handle and it turns. He nods to me and I press the button.

Theo flings the door open and we dash in. We are now in the stairwell of the first floor, and Theo gestures for me to release the button. I do. We look outside and the red line of the laser goes off.

Schools are creepy places at night. Somehow everything looks different, and all the usual sounds that accompany us as we walk the halls are absent. All we hear is the echoing of our footsteps. We head for the film and computer lab.

Once there, Theo makes easy work of the lock on the door and heads over to the workstation where we had been just this morning.

As he powers up the computer, Priti turns to me. "You know, this is kind of exciting."

I nod. "Theo really seems to have everything figured out."

Theo navigates to the folder where the uncorrupted files are. Suddenly I realize how he fooled Pablo. Right next to it is a folder with the corrupted files in it. He simply opened that folder after cleaning our files.

Theo inserts a flash drive and downloads our files. It takes about five minutes to move them all.

Theo checks the contents of the flash drive to confirm we've gotten what we need and then carefully deletes the files from the local server.

He powers down the computer and we prepare to leave.

None of us says a word as we head to the door. Theo nods to me and I text Lexie to use the pointer. A red beam of light can be seen through the window.

I push the button on the box and we head out the door into the cool autumn air.

Theo goes out first, followed by Priti, and then me.

We did it!

I turn to look at Priti, but she's looking beyond me, eyes wide.

I turn and try to make sense of what I'm seeing.

Holding Lexie's phone and the laser pointer isn't Lexie.

It's a large man in a black suit. He grabs my arm. And with his other gloved hand he gently pushes Priti's back.

"This way, please," he says pleasantly. I look ahead of us and see another man in a black suit who has Theo's backpack and his laptop.

And remarkably, Theo.

Who for the first time couldn't manage to vanish.

And standing next to them is . . . the last person I would have imagined . . .

My dad.

He doesn't look mad. Or upset. I can't read him.

Before I can figure it out, he gets into the front seat of an unmarked black van.

The two men push us into the van and I see the frightened face of Lexie in the very back seat.

Priti goes to sit next to her, and I follow.

The door to the van slides closed and we drive off into the night.

CHAPTER 31

Bad Rabbit

Okay, I got a little panicked. It wasn't some unmarked black government van.

It was just an Uber.

But I know I'm in deep trouble.

I figure I might as well ask the obvious question. "How did you know where we were?"

My dad doesn't turn around. "The GPS on your phone, Alex."

Theo shoots me a look with such fury I push back in my seat to avoid looking at him.

"You didn't turn your location off on your phone?" Theo says through clenched teeth.

Lexie pushes between us. "You never told us to do that."

"I didn't think I had to!" Theo says, clutching his head. "It's so *obvious*! Of all the—"

One of the two Men in Black raises his hand to his lips. "Okay, guys. Let's not fly off the handle. Plenty of time to talk when we get out."

"Where exactly are you taking us?" Priti asks. "My father knows people. You're not going to get away with this."

The other Man in Black puts down Theo's bag. "Miss Sharma, your parents have been informed that you are with us. Please calm down."

As we pull up to a building, Man in Black 1 turns to me and smiles. "Look familiar?"

Even in the dark, I can tell where we are.

It's my dad's office building. Where the commissioner's department is.

I lean forward. "Dad? These guys work with you?"

"Kind of," Dad says. "We'll explain once we're inside."

The door opens, and we stumble out of the van.

I see a blur of motion, and then I hear an *oomph*.

Man in Black 2 is breathing hard, but he has his hands firmly around Theo's skinny arms. He's marching him back to the group. "This one tried to make a run for it," he tells his partner.

Priti and Lexie look at me. None of us can believe Theo wasn't able to pull his disappearing act.

"Hey, Theo, don't you want your things back?" Man in Black 2 taunts, holding up his bag.

Theo grabs for it.

"Stop teasing him," Man in Black 1 says.

He turns to Theo. "Listen, Theo. We may need your help in there. This isn't whatever you think it is."

"How do you know what I think?" Theo says softly. His eyes are darting around.

The two men and my dad march us up to the door, which my dad unlocks.

We head in and get into the elevator. Man in Black 1 presses the button for the thirtieth floor.

"But, Dad, your office is on fifteen," I say.

Dad's voice is flat. "We're not going to my office."

The elevator doors open and we're faced with a thick glass door.

On it is a small ominous label, die-cut from a piece of matte-gray metal, like aluminum or something. It says GRU.

Theo's eyes widen. He turns to me. "GRU. That's the Russian secret police."

Man in Black 2 doesn't even bat an eye. "Yeah, we make jokes about that all the time. It actually stands for *government research unit.*"

Theo does *not* laugh.

Man in Black 1 swipes a keycard and the doors slide noiselessly open.

We walk down a carpeted hallway that leads to a large conference room.

The four of us enter and see row upon row of computers

that have been set up on long tables. There are men and women at each one, moving between them or taking something from a printer in the corner.

My dad walks over to his boss, Dan Rubin.

Why is everybody here?

After consulting with Mr. Rubin, my dad comes back to us.

"Kids, I'm sorry this had to be so dramatic, but we're dealing with a real crisis here," he says.

Lexie leans into me. "No kidding."

Then something occurs to my dad. "I guess I should introduce you to your new friends. This is Agent O'Connor and Agent Kelly. They work in District Attorney Freed's Fraud Unit."

"The Freed Fraud Unit?" I say, and stifle a laugh.

The girls crack up too.

My dad is not amused. "That's not funny, Alex."

"Oh, come on, Dad," I say. "Freed Fraud Unit. You have to admit it sounds silly."

Agent O'Connor has been busy getting chairs for us. "Yeah, we try not to use that. We're actually part of the cyber-crime division. Loaned out to District Attorney Freed."

"You're feds?" Theo says, sounding a little impressed.

"Yep. You wanna see my badge?" Agent Kelly says. He has two cans of soda in each large hand. "I thought you guys might be thirsty."

Agent Kelly leans down as we open our sodas, except for Theo.

"Relax, Theo, it's not drugged," he jokes.

Theo hands the can back. "That's what you say."

Agent Kelly nods. "No problem. But we're really on a little bit of a time crunch here. Let me tell you why you're here."

"That would be nice," Priti says.

"It's partly for your own protection, and partly because we need your help."

Now Theo is interested.

Agent O'Connor has gone to a laptop in the front of the room. Agent Kelly nods to him.

He presses a button and an image appears on the large screen mounted on the back wall.

On the screen are two words:

BAD RABBIT

Priti raises her hand. "Is this something to do with *Alice in Wonderland*?"

Theo snorts.

Agent Kelly turns to us. "Not exactly. Bad Rabbit is malicious software."

"Ransomware, to be exact," Theo says.

Agent O'Connor nods. "You want to tell us what you know about Bad Rabbit?"

Theo leans back in his chair. "Sure. It first showed up in 2017. Nasty worm. It basically encrypts all your data and when you try to restart any infected computer, it sends you a ransom note. You send the money in Bitcoin or some other crypto currency, and whoever set it up sends you the decryption key."

"You seem to know a lot about it," Agent Kelly says.

Theo laughs. "I mean, there are like dozens of videos on YouTube about it. And articles. And podcasts. Not hard if you're into this sort of thing."

I turn to my dad. "What does this have to do with us?"

My dad doesn't say anything, just turns to Agent Kelly.

Agent Kelly's eyes wander over each of us. "Okay. Your buddy here is correct that typically, ransomware asks for money. But this message was different."

On the screen, red letters pop up:

```
Oops! Your files have been encrypted.
If you see this text, your files are no
longer accessible.
You might have been looking for a way to
recover your files.

Don't waste your time. No one will be able
to recover them
Without our decryption service.

We guarantee that you will be able to
recover all your files safely.

All you need to do is submit to our demands
and get the decryption password.
```

Agent Kelly presses his clicker and a new screen appears.

```
Our demands are twofold:
First, the commission must recommend against
the continuation of the Court Street
Project.
```

I look over at Theo, who is chewing his thumbnail.
Agent Kelly fixes his gaze on me as he presses his clicker.
Then we see the second demand.

```
Second, all files and copies of files
associated with the student film "Persephone
in Anselmland" must be uploaded so we may
delete them.
```

"Alex, you're the only connection between these two demands," Agent O'Connor says. "So what have you got to say
about this?"

CHAPTER 32

That's What I Call a Plot Twist

My mouth moves, but nothing comes out.

Finally, I blurt out: "How am I supposed to know why our stupid little film got involved with some crazy ransomware scheme?"

"It's not actually stupid," Priti corrects me. "It's a very smart satire."

"That's good to know," Agent Kelly says, "but not really helpful."

Theo moves to the front of the room. He is clearly heading to one of the computer terminals. The two agents flank him on either side.

There seems to be a struggle and Theo falls back against Priti and Lexie and lands on the floor.

My dad steps in. "Stop it! I only agreed to this because you told me there would be no interrogation!"

Agent O'Connor looks genuinely confused. "We didn't touch him! I swear."

Theo looks up from the floor at Priti. I swear she gives him a small nod, but maybe she's just expressing concern.

"I just tripped, Mr. Davis. Everything's cool," Theo says as he gets up. "I was just curious about a few things."

Agent Kelly looks relieved. "Sure. Shoot."

Theo begins pacing. "First of all, why Bad Rabbit? I mean, no one has used that in years. It's usually defeated by any capable antivirus software."

"Believe me, we were asking the same thing," Agent O'Connor says.

All eyes are on Theo as he paces to the front of the room. "And that's not the only funny thing. How did it get onto the network in the first place?"

Agent Kelly looks annoyed. "You'd have to ask Commissioner Rubin."

Commissioner Rubin looks uncomfortable. "It seems someone turned off the antivirus software on one of the terminals."

"So someone who has access to the computers here," Theo continues. "And has a motive. Let's go down the list of suspects," Theo says as the agents and my dad and Commissioner Rubin gather around him.

I hear whispers and see that while Theo has been pacing and making his big speech, Priti and Lexie have snuck over to a computer terminal in the back row. They wave me over to join them. I go and immediately realize what happened.

When Theo "tripped," he slipped Priti the flash drive.

Which is now in the USB slot in the terminal, and they are trying to review the footage that we took.

"Let me do this," I say. "It'll be faster." I slide into the chair. "If they look this way, one of you can cause a diversion, right?"

Lexie and Priti nod.

"Just get on with it," Lexie hisses.

I navigate to the desktop. I've been in this office hundreds of times over the years and hope that just like in my dad's office, they have access to photo- and movie-editing software on the computers to put promotional material on the Web.

Luckily, they do. I open the program and get the footage loaded in.

"Which files should we start with?" Lexie asks.

Priti answers before I can. "The stuff we shot outside, right?"

I'm a little annoyed that she didn't let me answer, but since I've already gotten that file open, it's clear I knew it already.

"This scene has always bothered me," I tell them. "There's something distracting in the background."

I press the PLAY button and we watch Jensen in his rabbit costume.

Then we watch it again.

I hear Theo's voice in the corner. "Have you checked to

see if any money has been put in any employee accounts recently?"

Agent Kelly sounds like *he's* the seventh grader. "Of course we did! What do you think we are? Amateurs?"

Just a little longer, Theo.

I run through the same footage.

Lexie's finger pushes past me and onto the monitor. "Wait! I see what you're talking about. Behind Jensen? Run it back!"

I rewind and stop the playback when Lexie taps me on the shoulder. "There!"

She's got good eyes.

Priti leans in. I can smell the shampoo in her hair.

I know that's not really important right now, but it does smell really good.

"Can you zoom in on that frame?" Priti asks.

"I can try," I say.

I pull in and the image degrades.

But it's clear that *something* is going on behind Jensen.

Priti figures it out first.

"Now, as to motive," Theo is saying. "We have a number of possibilities. . . ."

Priti calls out, "How about bribery?"

All the men who have been surrounding Theo rush to our terminal.

Agent Kelly grimly looks at the screen and retrieves a cable from the center of the room and plugs it into the laptop.

The image appears on the screen above us, larger than life.

There are two men behind Jensen, who is hopping around in his rabbit ears. As they walk by, it is clear what is happening.

One is handing over an envelope. He's got a hoodie on. I have no idea who he is.

But the man he is handing the envelope to—even with a baseball cap jammed down on his head—is unmistakable.

Although he looks out of place not wearing his usual suit and tie, it is clearly our hardworking councilman Derek Randolph.

From across the room, Theo is shaking his head. "It sure took you guys long enough."

Agent Kelly turns to my dad and Commissioner Rubin. "The other guy. You know him."

Commissioner Rubin bites his lip. He nods at my dad. Clearly this is hard for them.

"That's Hugh Hewitt. He's got two buildings on Fulton Street," my dad tells them.

"So . . . ," Agent Kelly says.

Suddenly we're back in school, and Priti has to answer before anyone else. "I know! I know! If the Court Street Towers go up, it would be competition for him."

Commissioner Rubin nods. He sounds sad. "We told Randolph not to approve those Hewitt buildings. He uses substandard materials. He goes cheap. And he's up to his ears in debt. It was always a mystery as to why the councilman let them go through."

"Mystery solved," I say.

My dad shoots me a "please don't be smart" look.

"We don't know what's in that envelope," Agent O'Connor says.

"I think we have a good guess," Agent Kelly says. "If he was willing to go to such lengths to get this film."

"But the one thing I don't get," Commissioner Rubin says, "is how he found out. How did they learn about the film in the first place?"

I think back to the day we filmed outside. "We weren't exactly being discreet."

I move the file forward a few frames at a time.

On the screen, Hugh Hewitt looks up and a slimy expression appears on his face.

"I think he's looking at Priti," Lexie says with disgust.

His expression changes and he pulls the hoodie over his face and rushes past the camera. In the background, Randolph has crossed the street and is walking in the other direction.

"But they had to have someone inside Saint Anselm's to make this work," Theo declares. "That's where Randolph's old teacher comes in."

The agents turn and look at him.

Theo continues. "I couldn't figure out who had corrupted our files."

Lexie pushes forward. "Wait. I know this. Beaverton is the only one who could have done it. But he's an old guy. Do you really think he's that smart about computers?"

Agent Kelly has been frantically trying to take notes during all this. "He didn't have to. All he needed was access. They could provide him with the rest. All he had to do was run the program."

"They?" I ask.

"Remember I said Hewitt was deep in debt?" my dad says. "He wasn't financing those buildings with his own money. He was borrowing from banks in Russia, China, whoever would lend to him."

"And they didn't want to lose their money to a nicer, better built building any more than he did," adds Commissioner Rubin.

"But one thing I don't get," I say. "Once the files were corrupted, we made everyone think they were still corrupt. So how did Hewitt's people know you fixed them?"

Theo closes his eyes. Then he smacks himself on the head. "You idiot," he says to himself. "You never checked for a keylogger."

Agent Kelly tries to hide his smile behind his hand.

Agent O'Connor is less forgiving. I don't think he liked being showed up by a bunch of kids. "You didn't check for a keylogger? You? Superspy Schatten?"

Priti turns to me. "I know what they're talking about. It's a program that runs in the background and records every keystroke on a computer or a phone. I know because my parents put one on my older brother's phone when they thought he was getting into trouble."

"That's gross," Lexie says.

Priti nods. "I know, right? Total invasion of privacy!"

It sinks in. "Ooohh . . . ," I say. "So when Theo used his software to get the files back, they had a trail of his every movement."

"That's right, Einstein," Lexie says.

"How fourth grade of you," I respond automatically.

My dad checks his watch. "Okay, I think we know what our next steps are."

The agents are already making phone calls.

The commissioner looks at my dad wearily. "First thing in the morning, press conference, I guess?"

My dad pats him on the back. "Hey, that's your moment to shine, Dan."

The two men laugh.

Then my dad turns to me and my friends. "Let's get you home. You've got some work to do before the film festival."

Oh, right. Editing the final cut in time for Monday's event.

The reason for making the film in the first place.

It all seems so silly now, but I guess it will be nice to see Felix's face when we win the Golden Reel.

CHAPTER 33

The Fall of the House of Beaverton

So it turns out that doing the final cut of a ten-minute film is a lot harder than I thought it would be.

It's only ten minutes, Lexie texts me when I say I can't meet her on Sunday, having worked two days straight on trying to get this thing finished. "How long could that take?"

Well, there are a *lot* of things that go into it. Like making sure the dialogue is understandable.

"Remember," Pablo told us. "You might know your screen-play by heart, but your audience is hearing it for the first time."

It's also hard to know how to make something funny. Like should I put Persephone reacting to something she's hearing, or just keep watching Mr. Bergstrom with his silly voice?

And then there's the idea of music between scenes.

Nobody could agree on what to use, so we had to agree on something that none of us loved. But that's what my dad calls compromise. He says it happens all the time with buildings. The developer wants to build a sixty-story tower, and the commission's ecological impact report says it should be thirty for the area.

He said a bunch of other things, but I kind of stopped listening at that point.

I get it.

Okay, speaking of developers, Dad tells us at dinner that Agents O'Connor and Kelly paid a visit to Councilman Randolph's office with the footage, and he agreed to wear a wire to get evidence on Hewitt. And of course he's stepping down.

"To spend more time with his family," my mom says, which is apparently a big joke because that's what politicians who leave office because of some scandal say instead of "I have to resign because I got caught taking money from some sketchy dude."

"I'm sure Ricky will be thrilled to have him around," my dad says.

"Who is Ricky?" Violet asks.

"You've seen him," my dad says. "He's on Councilman Randolph's Christmas card every year."

Now I remember. It's funny because Councilman Randolph isn't even married or anything. His "family" consists of a big golden retriever named Ricky.

Immediately Violet turns the conversation to us getting a dog, which happens like every night.

I ask to be excused and go back to my room to finish the movie.

As I watch the scenes unfold, it all looks so silly and normal. Like everything that happened over the last few weeks was just a dream.

Or a movie?

/////

Pablo was both thrilled to have our film in the festival and baffled by what had occurred. Thankfully, when we screened the final cut for him, he actually laughed in a few places.

"Right under the wire!" he says, as he was just about to print out the program for tonight's showing.

The next few hours jump by, as everyone at school talks about the scandal at the city council.

Finally, it's showtime.

I arrive with my parents and Violet.

As we enter the ratty old auditorium at Saint Anselm's, there is an excited buzz as kids, parents, and teachers pour in. The seats begin to fill up, and my folks find three together in the center section. They know I don't want to sit with them. I'd be too uncomfortable watching their reaction.

I see Lexie waving at me from across the room. I join her and see that there are sheets of paper with FILMMAKERS printed on them, reserving seats.

"I have these saved," Lexie says.

"You can't sit here," I tell her. "You're not a filmmaker."

Lexie's face drops. "But I helped."

Theo has somehow materialized in the seat beside her. "Let her stay. There wouldn't be a film without her."

"Fine with me," I say, "but if they ask you to leave, you're gonna have to leave because you're not *really* a—"

"Give it a rest, Alex," Lexie growls. "I get it."

I look over and see Priti sitting with Jensen and her real friends. They are chatting and taking selfies. She doesn't even look in our direction.

"I guess things are back to normal," I say.

Lexie follows my gaze and I notice she looks sad too. "That's the way it goes sometimes, Xan, ol' pal."

I laugh in spite of myself. "I don't know what I was thinking."

"You thought you were a Xan," Lexie says, "but you are just an Alex. I like Alex better anyway."

Theo looks like he just thought of something. "Oh! Hey, good job on the editing. The movie looks really good!"

He gives me a thumbs-up.

"Wow, coming from you, that makes me feel pretty great," I say, since I know if he thought it stank he would have told me.

"I still think using that boppy-doopy music in the Tweedledee scene kind of ruins it, but that was Priti's choice, so . . . ," he adds.

I nod. "Yeah, totally."

Actually, it was my choice, but I sure am not going to remind him.

Pablo has moved to the front of the stage area. Behind him is a large screen. Not as big as the one in the commissioner's office, but still pretty impressive.

He is wearing a tuxedo jacket over a T-shirt. And a baseball cap. I mean, if he hadn't, we'd have been disappointed.

"At least he's not wearing a top hat," Lexie whispers to me.

Pablo gives a whistle and slowly people sit down and the room falls silent.

"First of all, thank you all for coming to this, the fiftieth annual Focus on Student Film Festival!" he proclaims.

We all clap and whoo-whoo.

Pablo takes a piece of paper from his pocket.

Lexie looks over at me and grins.

It's kind of cool that the four of us are the only students in the room who know what Pablo is going to say next.

"I know most of you are surprised to see me up here, instead of Mr. Beaverton. For fifty years this has been his baby," he begins. "Sadly, tonight he can't join us."

There is a loud gasp from a lot of the students. Then a loud murmur of concern as kids are clearly trying to figure out what's going on.

Pablo waves his hands again. "Please! I just want to assure everyone that Mr. Beaverton is fine. He's not sick. He just is unable to attend tonight's presentation."

"Yeah, unable," Theo snickers. "That's a nice way of putting it."

Instead of going to trial and possibly facing jail time for aiding and abetting Hugh Hewitt, Mr. Beaverton agreed to plead guilty to a lesser charge and do community service. But once Director of School Vincent found out what had happened, Beaverton was discharged (that's a nice way of saying he had his butt fired). He apparently asked that he be allowed to come to the festival tonight, but I'm happy to say that was *not* going to happen.

Pablo clears his throat and reads from his prepared statement. "'Because of circumstances that I am unable to share with you, as of today Mr. Beaverton will no longer be teaching at Saint Anselm's.'"

There is consternation from Beaverton's students. A few boos are heard.

"'I will be assuming the role of head of the film department and will be joined next semester by a new film studies teacher, who many of you know already.'"

He gestures to his right and is joined by Jamila Jameson. I remember when she was hired, she was the first black history teacher Saint Anselm's ever had, which is both really sad that it took so long and really great because I had her in fifth grade and she is awesome.

There are cheers for her (she's really popular), and she waves to the kids.

"I didn't know she made films," Lexie says.

"She had a short film at the Sundance Film Festival that won some sort of award," Theo says.

I turn to him. "You're amazing. How do you know that?"

Theo holds up his phone and waves it in my face. "I just googled her. You should try it sometime."

Okay, so I'm not superspy material.

"And now," Pablo says, "let's meet our judges!"

He gestures to a small table that's been set up in front of the screen.

"'First, please welcome the writer, producer, and star of the hit TV series *Girl Problems*. Hannah Krausz, class of 2003!'"

A small woman with short hair framing a round face enters the auditorium. There are squeals from the girls and even some of the boys.

"'And joining Hannah is the director of *Mexican Standoff* and the new superhit *Paperback Original* . . . Saint Anselm's class of '96 . . . Cody Fantano!'"

A tall rangy guy in a tight-fitting leather jacket bounds into the room, pumping his fist and chewing gum.

Now it's the boys' turn to hoot, and he accepts high fives from some of them as he makes his way to his seat. He and Hannah nod at one another.

"'They have graciously taken time from their busy schedules to come and judge this festival,'" Pablo says. "'And determine . . . which film is the . . . winner . . . of the Golden Reel.'"

Clearly, saying those words is really hard for him. We know how much he hates the thought of films competing against each other.

He puts the paper away and looks down.

He takes a deep breath.

"Uh-oh," I say to Lexie.

Pablo crosses his arms in front of his chest. "I just . . . have to say something. Mr. Beaverton created this program and deserves all the credit for making film studies what it is at Saint Anselm's."

"He was the best, man!" Cody Fantano yells out from the sidelines. "I learned more from him than any of the teachers I had at film school!"

I should mention that he said a curse word before *teachers,* but I am not going to repeat it. There was some coughing in the audience as clearly some parents had never seen a Cody Fantano movie. For him, that was actually tame.

"Yes, well," Pablo continues, "that being said, we had our differences. As such, this will be the last year we will be awarding the Golden Reel."

The room falls silent. Hannah Krausz nods enthusiastically.

Pablo looks at his feet. "I just feel that kids shouldn't be worrying about winning prizes. They should just make the best film they can. And that should be reward enough."

Cody Fantano pops a bubble. "Too bad, man. Winning the Golden Reel was the thing that got me hooked on making movies."

Hannah Krausz leans forward. "You go, Pablo. I *didn't* win, and see where it got me!"

Pablo smiles and lets out a deep breath. "Okay. That's for next year. This year, we have seven very different but equally brilliant films to show you. And one of them will be awarded the Golden Reel!"

There is applause, and Pablo goes to sit down next to the judges as the lights dim.

I check the program. Our film is seventh. Right after Felix's.

Does that mean they're saving the best for last?

CHAPTER 34

The Competition

The first film starts and it's Beverly, Ramona, and Zuzu's *No Talent Show.*

I could make a snide comment and say that the title is fitting, but there are actually some pretty good scenes between two competing girls who both want to sing the same song. They got two girls from the high school to be in it, and they are really funny at being bad singers. But seriously, that was all that it was.

At the end, there is polite clapping from the parents and whooping from the girls' friends.

The next one is *The Haunting: Summer House* by Tony and Fronk. It's supposed to be scary, but mostly it's showing off Fronk's parents' summer house in East Hampton.

I turn to Lexie. "Is the house killing them one by one?"

She looks back with her hand over her mouth. "I dunno. I think so, or maybe it's a symbol for something?"

When one of the kids is supposed to fall down a flight of stairs, there's a cut, and it's so obvious that they just threw a big doll down instead that giggles are heard throughout the room.

"That's not a good sign," Theo says, and nudges Lexie.

It ends with the camera panning across this enormous gourmet kitchen. I swear I hear all the parents in the audience go "Oooh!" when they see it.

"If there was an award for biggest kitchen flex, I think we have a winner," Lexie says.

The house was definitely the star of that movie.

Next is *Face Your Fears and Win the Gold!,* which is of course Jojo and her crew's movie.

There is a really nice slow-motion shot of Jojo running for the vault.

Then another one of her teammates cheering her on.

Then another one as she falls.

And another one as she writhes in pain.

"Is this whole movie in slow motion?" Lexie asks me.

"I don't know what you're talking about," I say with a straight face. "It's totally normal speed. Maybe your brain has slowed down."

She pokes me in the ribs.

They found some unbelievably corny inspirational music to use, but I have to admit the scenes of her trying to get over her fears are pretty well edited. The problem is that Jojo isn't really an actress. It's awfully clear in the scenes where she's supposed to be crying that they just dripped water on her face. But when she nails the vault, there is wild clapping from the audience (I think it was started by Jojo, but that's okay). It ends, of course, on a freeze-frame of her holding her medal aloft.

I sneak a look at the judges.

Hannah is dutifully taking notes on each movie. Cody looks bored.

Next is *The Battle for the Serpents,* which is Ralph, Noel, and Cammi's movie.

It has a *very* long rolling text sequence that supplies all the plot that we're supposed to know before the movie starts. It's read by Lucretia Lopez, the chairperson of the theater department. She is very, um, *dramatic.* Still, it's hard to keep track of who is chasing who, whose family is fighting what battle, and why this whole serpent thing is so important.

After that, there is a scene in an "inn," which is just some-body's basement. The costumes are pretty amazing (Cammi really is a genius), but then Jojo jumps into the scene and starts whacking the other kids with her sword. I don't even know how they talked her into doing it (I think she's played the role-playing game with them before), but it doesn't have the desired effect. You can hear a lot of coughing as parents try hard not to laugh.

It kind of falls apart at that point, but victory is had and the world is saved, so yay?

Theo nudges me. "What the heck was that?"

I join the polite applause. "You got me."

Noel is standing up and bowing, while Ralph and Cammi are trying to pull him back to his seat.

Next is *Crotch Tape*.

I mean, not much to say about this.

Nathan and Mateo didn't even bother to get anyone else to be in it.

There are shrieks of laughter from the kids in the audience, and I see some of the parents shaking their heads by the time one of the boys gets hot sauce poured into his underpants.

I hear one loud barking laugh over in the corner and see Cody Fantano having the time of his life.

Lexie looks at me and shakes her head. "I guess people love that sort of thing."

"Lexie, you were laughing pretty hard at some of those *things*," I tell her.

"You have to admit, the hot sauce was epic," she says.

I bite my lip as Felix's film begins.

Builder of Lies shows up on the screen.

He got Mr. Anthony from the high school office to play a scheming developer. They intercut scenes of the meeting that he shot when we visited the Building Commission. Mr. Anthony is literally rubbing his hands together and saying "Heh-heh-heh . . ."

I wonder what Mr. Tolliver is thinking. I crane my neck to see if he is here, but it's hard to make out people's faces in the dark.

There are scenes of Felix and other kids handing out leaflets and getting people to sign petitions.

Ultimately, the crooked building commissioner is found out (they don't say how; they just show a fake newspaper headline. I guess he couldn't come up with a plot), and the building is canceled. The kids celebrate and it all feels very inspiring, since in Felix's and his friends' world things are black-and-white and the bad guys always lose.

I mean, it's not like Felix was *wrong* about the crooked developer. And he did make a film about *something.* I'm just saying he picked the wrong developer, that's all.

When it's over, there is a huge amount of clapping and whistles. I don't know if Felix's parents brought friends with them or if people were genuinely moved by the film.

Just as our film is about to start, I smell something really nice over my right shoulder.

It's Priti's shampoo.

She's come over to watch our film with us.

"I was too nervous to sit with my friends," she says.

Lexie reaches over and squeezes her hand. "Good luck!"

Priti gives a small smile. "Thanks."

Now, you see, if I had done that, Priti would have given me a look like "Ew."

I mean, I don't know that for *sure,* but I'm pretty sure.

I am definitely not going to squeeze Theo's hand.

Especially since he's currently chewing his thumbnail.

"I think ours is better than all of the other ones," Priti whispers to me.

"Definitely," I whisper back.

The titles appear, and the scenes that I slaved over for weeks editing finally play in front of the audience.

There are lots of laughs throughout, especially since Persephone is so good at reactions and at knowing just how long to wait before saying the punch line. She really is talented, and we were so lucky to get her.

When Mr. Halverson (who is *famous* for being the hardest grader in the English department) plays Humpty Dumpty and says, "When I use a word, it means just what I choose it to mean—neither more nor less," that gets a really big reaction from the high schoolers in the audience. And when Director of School Vincent yells "Off with their heads!" even the parents clap.

Out of the corner of my eye, I see Priti watching all of this. The lights of the screen bounce off her perfect features, and she has a beautiful smile on her face.

"Hey! Earth to Alex!"

I am aware of a voice next to me and turn to see Lexie snapping her fingers in front of my eyes.

"Stand up!" she orders me.

I guess I got lost there for a moment and didn't realize the movie is over. The room has erupted in cheers, and I see that Persephone is standing up and waving and now is pointing at Priti and me and—

Theo is nowhere to be seen. Of course.

CHAPTER 35

Welcome to the Reel World

As the lights come up, Pablo rushes onstage. "Our judges will now confer and make their decision. Please feel free to mingle—we'll let you know when they're ready to make their announcement."

There is a general shuffling of feet and burble of voices as parents rush to congratulate their geniuses and kids tell their friends why their film is the best.

I look over to see that Priti has gone to join her folks. Her mom is in a bright red scarf and chic outfit, standing out even in this group of somewhat fashionable parents. Priti has brought Lexie with her, and I watch as she is clearly explaining who she is, and I hear her mom loudly say Isabel's name and hug Lexie.

I scan the room looking for my folks. I finally spot them behind a huge group of students who have surrounded Persephone, like worshippers at her shrine. I mean, she was really good in our movie, but it's not like she made it or anything.

As I pass her, she's in the middle of taking another selfie with one of her fans.

"Thanks again," I tell her, with all the genuine graciousness I can muster. "We couldn't have made it without you."

"Duh," Persephone says. "My name is in the title!"

All the kids laugh like she's said the wittiest thing in the entire history of the English language.

I want to say "You're welcome," but I am too classy for that. I just move on.

I discover my parents are talking to a pleasant-looking couple. The man is small and thin and wears a baggy suit and open-collared shirt. He has long gray hair and steel-rimmed glasses. His narrow face looks familiar. The woman is slightly rounder, in a comfortable sweater and has close-cropped hair.

Mom spots me. "Oh, there he is! Congratulations, sweetie! We're so proud of you!"

She kisses me on the cheek and then gestures to the couple. "We've got to meet the Schattens!"

Mr. Schatten extends his hand and shakes mine warmly. "Hey! You must be Alex! Dare Schatten. So glad to finally meet you!"

Mrs. Schatten gives me a big smile, and I am not making this up.

She hugs me. "We're so happy Theo's found some friends at Saint Anselm's."

Dad has been busy bribing Violet with a chocolate chip cookie (this is not their first school event) and joins the conversation. "Your son's quite an amazing kid."

Mr. Schatten grins. "They're all amazing kids, right?"

Mrs. Schatten looks behind me. "I'm sorry . . . but are you Lexie?"

I turn and see that Lexie has actually left Priti's side. She waves shyly.

"The famous Lexie!" Mrs. Schatten exclaims, and dives in and gives her a hug.

Over her shoulder, Lexie is giving me a "what the heck is going on?" look and I just grin.

"That was really a fantastic film you guys did," Mr. Schatten says, "even though we didn't get a lot of the jokes, being new to the school and all."

I am still processing that Theo's parents are totally not what I expected at all. "Oh, thanks. Theo was really great to work with."

I mean, if you can't lie to someone's parents, who *can* you lie to, right?

"They literally couldn't have made it without him," Lexie adds, which *is* true.

"From what Alex tells us, he's quite a computer whiz," Mom says.

Mr. Schatten frowns. "No more than any other kid his age, I imagine."

Is it possible they don't know about Theo?

"He knows a whole lot more than some of the teachers here," Lexie says.

Mrs. Schatten laughs. "You're very nice to say that, Lexie."

"I guess he learned a lot about hacking and computer security from you," I say.

Mr. Schatten looks confused. "From me? I don't know about that stuff."

Now it's my turn to look confused. "Isn't the name of your company Schatten Infosec?"

Mrs. Schatten leans in and pats her husband on the shoulder. "Oh, honey, it's that typo on your website."

"Right," he says, sighing. "My company is Schatten Info*seek*. We do research for companies that are interested in buying real estate to build their headquarters. Nothing so glamorous as computer security."

"He's more of a real estate agent than a secret agent," Mrs. Schatten says.

"Well, we can't all be superspies like Lexie and Alex here," my mom says. "Or Theo, of course."

Mr. and Mrs. Schatten look confused.

My dad bites his lip. "Umm . . . did Theo not tell you?"

Mr. Schatten shakes his head. "Please tell us Theo didn't do anything . . . irresponsible."

"Again," Mrs. Schatten adds.

"Not at all!" Dad says. "To the contrary! Theo was incredibly helpful in—"

There is a loud banging noise, and we turn to see Pablo gesturing for everyone to take their seats.

"We'll tell you afterward," my dad promises as the Schattens rush off to find their seats.

Lexie and I head back to our places.

"I did not expect that," she says, and I nod.

We sit down and Theo is already there.

"We met your parents," I tell him.

He makes a sour face. "Oh, yeah. I forgot they were coming."

"They seem really nice," Lexie says.

Theo looks away from us. "Oh, they're just peachy."

"I don't think he liked being busted," I say to Lexie.

"Who was busted?" Priti asks, joining us.

"I'll text you," Lexie promises.

Priti nods and we turn our attention to the stage.

Hannah and Cody are standing with Pablo.

I can't tell from the expression on his face if he's happy or not. He just looks overwhelmed.

"Once again, to announce the winners of this year's Golden Reel, please join me in welcoming back Hannah Krausz and Cody Fantano!"

Pablo leads the applause and runs off the stage.

Hannah Krausz clears her throat and takes out a piece of paper with her notes scribbled all over it.

Cody Fantano takes out another piece of gum, unwraps it, and puts it in his mouth.

"First off, let's have one more round of applause for all

this year's films," she begins. "Each one was spectacular in its own way!"

"Totally." Cody nods.

"So it was particularly difficult to pick a winner from among them."

Yeah, yeah. We know. Just get on with it.

Hannah and Cody share a look. "So this year . . . we have . . . a tie!"

Lexie, Theo, Priti, and I exchange looks. Well, a tie is better than nothing.

"Between *Builder of Lies* . . . and . . ."

I start to get up.

Then Cody reads the other name. "*Crotch Tape!*"

I watch in astonishment as Felix and his troupe run up, followed by Nathan and Mateo.

As the cheers subside, I notice that Priti has gone off to join her friends.

Hannah turns to Felix. "We were so impressed with your use of film to spotlight and fight social injustice."

Felix beams and waves the Golden Reel over his head.

Hannah then addresses Nathan and Mateo. "And we were equally blown away by your use of the classic comedy tradition."

They all stand there looking awkward, and Pablo rushes back onstage.

"So that's our show! Let's hear it for our winners! And good night!"

There is applause and people rush for the doors.

Lexie grabs my hand and pulls me aside.

"I don't care what they say. You guys did amazing."

"Thanks, Lexie," I say. "But you left someone out."

Lexie thinks for a second. "Okay, *we* did amazing."

I smile. "That's better."

Suddenly, I realize why Violet loves her Elsa doll.

My parents are in their coats. Dad is carrying Violet. She's seven, which I think is a little old for this. But I'm not the one carrying her, so I don't say anything.

"Sorry, buddy," my dad says.

"Remember what Pablo said," my mom says, deciding now is the time for a life lesson.

I grit my teeth. "I know, Mom. It's *fine*."

I'm about to say more when this dark-haired woman who looks vaguely familiar comes up. I think she's going to say something about the film, but instead she goes right to my dad.

"Mr. Davis? Alex?" she asks.

"Yes," he says, and gives her a look of recognition. "Ginia? From the *Times*?"

Her face breaks out in a big smile. "Yes! You remember!"

She turns to my mom and reaches out her hand. There is a business card in it. "Ginia Dellarobbia. I write for the *New York Times*. My son's a sixth grader with Adam Tolliver."

She looks at my dad. "So I heard there is quite a story behind the Hewitt indictment. I'd love to chat with you about it."

"Well," my dad says, "I have to check with my department . . ."

Ginia waves him off. "I've already got the green light from

both Commissioner Rubin's office and the Office of Public Affairs. They say you can tell me everything."

My dad laughs. "Well, I'm sure you'll want to hear from these two as well."

Ginia nods. "Of course. I want to hear *everything*. I'll reach out to you tomorrow and we can set it up."

She goes off into the crowd, and Lexie and I look at each other.

"The *New York Times*, huh?" Lexie sniffs.

"That'll make Felix's head explode," I say.

"Count me out," a voice says.

Theo has popped up out of the crowd. "Say whatever you want. Just don't mention me, please."

Lexie puts her hands on her hips. "Theo, how can we tell the story without you?"

"I'm asking you. Just find a way of keeping me out of it," he says.

He sounds so genuinely anxious that I don't know what to do. "Okay, Theo, we'll . . . just make up a little bit of it. Okay?"

He pushes his hair out of his eyes and meets my gaze. "You promise?"

"Yes, Theo, I'll make sure," I say.

He relaxes. But only a little. "Okay."

My mom doesn't wait for introductions. "So you're the famous Theo."

Theo looks suspicious. "How did she know that?"

I sigh. "Maybe because she overheard Lexie calling you 'Theo.'"

"Oh, right," Theo says. "Nice to meet you."

My mom gives him a little bow. "Nice to meet you too."

My dad shifts Violet to his other shoulder. "Sorry, but we really have to get going. This one is up way past her bedtime."

We walk down the stairs to the front of the building. As we get outside, I realize something.

I look around. "Hey, Theo. Where are your parents?"

"They went on ahead. They do that," he answers.

My mom checks her watch. "It's a little late. Would you like us to walk you home?"

"Oh, no, that won't be necessary," Theo says. "I don't want to inconvenience you."

Now my dad is concerned. "I'll just drop this little one off and then I can walk you. No problem."

"Or we can put you in a car," my mom suggests. "Where do you live?"

"Please!" Theo begs. "I can get home by myself."

We watch as he runs off into the night.

We catch glimpses of him as he passes under streetlights, getting smaller and smaller as he finally vanishes into the darkness of the Brooklyn night, the sounds of his steps in the silent air getting fainter and fainter.

We don't know it yet, but this will be the last we ever see of Theo Schatten.

EPILOGUE

Was it wrong of me to assume that when Ginia Dellarobbia came over to the house to interview me, she would want to know about how I ended up taking film class? Or that the reason I was so good at editing was my accident at skate camp? I mean, that stuff was pretty important to the story.

Right?

Well, she didn't seem to think so. She kept asking about Priti, and how Lexie got involved, and how I knew them, and spent most of the time talking to Dad about who he thought was going to run in the special election to replace Councilman Randolph.

Of course Violet was acting all cute as a button, and Ginia

has a little girl who's also in her class, so she and Mom talked a whole lot about Saint Anselm's and how they have to get the girls together over Christmas break.

I should have figured something was going on, because Ginia didn't have a photographer with her, but I guess I assumed they would come later or maybe the story wouldn't have pictures.

Ha!

So the story gets printed (in the Sunday paper, the one everyone reads) and splashed across the front page of the Metropolitan section is a photo of Priti and Lexie sitting in front of a laptop in Priti's fancy apartment with the view behind them.

The whole article was all about these two "hacker girls" who took down a corrupt city official. The only time I'm mentioned in the entire article is as "the son of Deputy Commissioner Davis, a classmate of Priti and Lexie, who brought them together as part of a class project."

I don't even get my name in the paper.

Okay, to be fair, Lexie and Priti *did* figure out most of Hewitt's scheme, and "superspy" Theo did ask not to be mentioned in the article. But still!

And the worst part? At the end of the article, showing how important it is to have role models like Lexie and Priti, a "seven-year-old second grader" named Violet Davis is quoted as saying, "I want to be just like Lexie and Priti when I grow up!" As if *they're* grown-ups.

She gets to be mentioned in the article and I don't?

And of course Priti and Lexie get invited to be on the *Today* show. At least I got to go with them. Now, that was cool, even if the hosts kept directing most of the questions to the girls, who talked all about how we figured out the whole bribery scheme while making a student film. Lexie made a point of saying my name a few times, which was really nice of her.

To be honest, I hate how my voice sounds, especially when it's recorded, so that part wasn't all bad.

What was totally weird was that I had to wear makeup. I also wore my only nice shirt.

Priti looked pretty much the same as always, but Lexie looked totally different. She wore a cool vintage-looking sweater and had her hair styled by somebody. And she was wearing makeup too. To be honest, it took me a minute to realize it was her.

"You look very nice," I told her.

"Like as opposed to how I usually look, is that what you mean?" Lexie answered.

I never seem to be able to say the right things. "No, it's not that. You just—"

"I was just psyching you," Lexie laughed. "You're so cute when you're flustered."

I didn't know what to say to that, so I said, "You too," which didn't make any sense, but then they called us into the studio, so I didn't have to deal with it.

A few days later, I'm sitting in the living room thinking all sorts of things, like what a weird year this has already been, with everything that's happened, and what Lexie meant when she said I looked cute, when my phone vibrates. I look down and it's a text.

From Lexie.

Hey. I'm outside. Wanna hang?

I run to the front door. Then I count to thirty. I don't want to seem too overanxious.

I mean, she's been practically living with Priti. She can wait a little longer.

I open the door and she's standing right there.

"What did you do, count to thirty or something?" she asks.

Her face is makeup free and she's back in her old T-shirt.

It's almost as if none of it had happened.

But of course, it did.

And it changed everything.

"So . . . did you hear about Cody Fantano's next project?" Lexie says as we settle in on the stoop in front of my house.

I grab a corn chip from the open bag in her lap. "Let me guess. He's going to make a big-budget version of *Crotch Tape*."

"You're close," Lexie says wearily. She pulls up an entertainment website on her phone.

There's a big headline: FANTANO TO HELM HACKER GIRLS MOVIE! INSPIRED BY REAL EVENTS!

"Wait, what?" I stare at the screen. "He can't do that. I mean, doesn't he have to get our approval or pay us anything?"

"Apparently not," Lexie says. "According to the article, he's going to do 'his own take' on our story."

I sit there, stunned. "Unbelievable."

We look out in silence at the early December sky darkening.

Now or never.

"Um . . . Lexie, you know, uh . . . I feel weird saying this to you."

She looks at me. "Just say it."

"It's just that, I need to tell you something. When I saw you in the studio, I noticed . . ."

Lexie laughs. "I know what you're going to say. I told them I didn't want any makeup, but the makeup lady said I'd wash out on camera and needed at least a little foundation and blush. Then she told me my lips would disappear if she didn't put something on them. Then I looked in the mirror and I saw this circus clown staring back at me."

"Um, actually, I thought you looked good," I say.

Lexie's eyes widen. "You did? So you weren't just saying that? I really didn't look weird?"

"No, you looked really nice," I tell her. "But not because of the makeup. You looked confident. Like you do now. Like . . . you always do. You know . . . cool."

"Huh," Lexie says. She stares at her sneaker and starts playing with the laces.

I take a deep breath. "Lexie, it's kind of funny. We have so much in common. Even the same name, you know? And going to school together for all these years . . ."

She doesn't look up. "Yeah?"

She's not making this easier.

"I just never thought about this before. But after everything we've just gone through . . . you know how sometimes you change your feelings about someone?"

Lexie looks me right in the eyes. "Hold on. Are you . . . like suggesting that we . . . like, go out together? I mean like be a *couple*?"

Now it's my turn to look at my sneakers. "Yeah, that was the general idea."

I sneak a look at Lexie, who is smiling from ear to ear.

All of a sudden, she hugs me so hard I almost fall over.

I take this as a good sign.

Then, when she lets go, I see the expression on her face. There is something about the way she is looking at me as she shakes her head and gives a small laugh.

"Oh, Alex, you are the best . . . but here's the thing."

She stops and is about to say something. And stops herself. Like three times.

I can't stand it. "Just say it, Lexie."

"You know how you . . . feel . . . when you look at Priti?" she asks.

I shift uncomfortably. "Yeah, I think I know what you mean."

Lexie cups her chin in her hands and stares out onto the street. "That's how *I* feel when I look at Priti too."

It takes me a minute, because I am a total dim bulb.

"Wait, so you like girls?" I ask.

"That's the general idea," Lexie says, not looking at me.

"Huh," I say. "How come you never told me?"

She turns and is the old Lexie. "Alex, seriously? What was I supposed to say? 'So Mr. Halverson sure gave us a lot of homework today, right? And, oh by the way, I'm gay.'"

"That's true," I say.

We sit in silence for a minute.

"So . . . you like girls?" I say.

"Yes, Alex. I like girls."

I can't help it.

"Well, I like girls too! See, I told you we had a lot in common!"

Lexie bursts out laughing and hugs me again.

This time I hug her back.

ACKNOWLEDGMENTS

It would be such a lazy, easy cliché to say that making a book is like making a movie, in that both require a team of talented and driven individuals working together to make the author's vision a reality.

So call me lazy and easy (it wouldn't be the first time).

Seriously, this project was moved forward because of the trust that my stalwart publisher, Beverly Horowitz, had in me at a time when none of us knew what the future would bring. I hope that trust was merited.

I need to mention that although the editor of my first three books, the brilliant Kate Sullivan, has moved on to use her gift of getting the finest work out of other lucky writers, her lessons will always stay with me, and I am a better writer for having worked with her.

Alison Romig, my new editor, while youthful in both years and spirit, was exactly the right person for this project and for me. She pushed me and the book to be our best with enthusiasm, humor, and an unerring eye for what needed to be cut and what needed to be clarified.

As always, a low bow of thanks and gratitude goes to my brilliant agent, Holly Root, who has the ability to say just the right thing when I need to hear it the most. May she always be in my corner!

When there are errant misspellings or other errors, I know I can count on my intrepid copyeditors (Carrie Andrews and Colleen Fellingham), who are the Priti and Lexie of the project, spotting every missed detail and making sure the guilty party is vanquished.

And as the music plays me off, I must quickly give a shoutout to cover designer Michelle Cunningham, who put up with my suggestions, and brilliant cover artist Louie Chin, whose work probably made you pick up the book in the first place.

Wait! Of course I can't forget to thank the real stars of my reality show:

My wife, Melissa Iwai, artist, author, and love of my life. She of the sympathetic ear and critical eye, and coproducer of:

Our best creation, our son, Jamie, whose work as a student filmmaker inspired this book. Jamie has been known to say to me "Will you *stop* using my life in your books?"

Seeing as he's finishing high school, I think he's safe now.

And finally,

To my mother, Joan Markell, who, having lost her husband of sixty-four years, then got through the extraordinary pandemic year of 2020 with resilience, strength, and good humor, all my love.

Mom, I would say you are my biggest fan *and* my harshest critic, but I'm not sure about the last part. I try to stay off Goodreads.

ABOUT THE AUTHOR

DENIS MARKELL, a devoted cinephile (that means he loves movies), has been a playwright and a composer/lyricist and has written for several sitcoms. He cowrote a play with Joan Rivers, which was produced in Los Angeles and London. He can be seen in the background of her critically acclaimed documentary, looking optimistic. With all that, the credit that seems to impress people the most is that he wrote an episode of *Thundercats.* His debut novel, *Click Here to Start,* was a Junior Library Guild Selection. His second novel, *The Game Masters of Garden Place,* was a *Time for Kids* Buzzworthy Book of the Summer. *The Ghost in Apartment 2R* was a Winter Kids' Indie Next List Top 10 Pick.

A lifelong resident of Brooklyn Heights, he lives in a small apartment with his wife and son and an extremely photogenic Shiba Inu named Nikki.